Murder Among Friends

MISS MARKHAM MYSTERY SERIES
BOOK ONE

JULIET E. SIDONIE

Murder Among Friends

MISS MARKHAM MYSTERY SERIES
BOOK ONE

JULIET E. SIDONIE

Murder Among Friends — A Miss Markham Mystery

ISBN 978-1-733044-1-7 (hardcover) — 978-1-733044-2-4 (paperback)

Copyright © 2024 by Miss Markham Mysteries, LLC

This book is dedicated to Doris Markham, our inspiration and role model. Yes, she is a real person who may not have lived all of these adventures, but with her adventurous spirit, she could have!

Acknowledgments

We would like to thank our families and friends for their support, suggestions, and help. Thanks especially go to our beta readers Elden Dilks, Joyce Henkins, Kristie Zorn, Allen and Tiffany Winningham, Jo Ann Day, Gail Schartel, Racheal Shatswell, Greg Reilly, and Alina Guerra, along with a multitude of others who offered their suggestions for improvements, to include Rebecca Blocksome and Sara McClure. Thank you also to Lenora Dilks for her book cover artwork.

More Information

At the back of the book, you will find additional information, including a dictionary of the slang used and references to newspaper articles that inspired the stories. For more historical tidbits, visit our website at MissMarkham Mysteries.com.

Table of Contents

List of Characters

Deloris "DeDe" Markham – A brunette with violet eyes, a knockout figure, and good-looking gams, Deloris knows there's more to the world than the small town she grew up in. Her friends and family call her DeDe because as a child she stuttered and couldn't say her name.

Paul Sullivan – An employee at the soda fountain at Poppy's Paradise Park. Paul looks straight from the Emerald Isle, with sandy colored hair, freckles, and blue eyes.

Thelma Webb – Deloris's two-times-divorced older sister who has two children she is raising on her own. To help make ends meet, she rents rooms in her house to single females.

Walter McKinley – Walter is Thelma's second ex-husband, a sucker for get-rich-quick schemes. He pops up at her boarding house from time to time, begging for money and a meal.

George "Brown" Nelson – A friend of Paul Sullivan's. George always looks out for his little brother, Gordon, since the two of them only have each other.

Gordon "Baby Face" Nelson – Also a friend of Paul Sullivan's. Gordon is George's younger brother. Gordon is angry at the world and always ready to get into a fight, but his older brother can usually calm him down.

Wanda Phillips – An older boarder at Thelma's boarding house, Wanda works as a bank teller. She is a widow who has a son named Terry.

Terrence "Terry the Terror" Phillips –The only child of Wanda Phillips. Terry can be friendly, but Wanda has spoiled him so much that he throws temper tantrums if he can't get what he wants. He has been in jail a few times, but not long enough to learn anything.

~ POPPY'S PARADISE PARK EMPLOYEES ~

Mr. O'Brien – Manager of Poppy's Paradise Park.

Stella – Deloris's co-worker, a lifeguard at the Crystal Pool.

Trudie – Deloris's co-worker, she works at a nearby concession stand.

Leon Iraklidis – Soda fountain repair fellow.

~ KANSAS CITY POLICE DEPARTMENT EMPLOYEES ~

Jim "Big Jim" Anderson – A detective at the Kansas City Police Department. Big Jim is over six feet tall with brown hair and green eyes. He is a former Marine who has mastered the art of the intimidating stare.

Carolyn Bechtel - The assistant coroner at the Kansas City Police Department. Carolyn is an attractive woman with short brown hair and soft blue eyes.

Sergeant Ted Cox – Front desk sergeant at the police station.

Elden Denton – Captain of the Kansas City Police Department's downtown branch. Elden is about fifty years old, in good shape for his age, and almost bald with the typical patch of semi-circled gray hair and deep blue eyes. Captain Denton has seen the best and the worst of humanity over his twenty-five years on the police force.

Austin Martin – A childhood friend of Deloris's who graduated from Jameson the year before her. Their mothers were good friends so Austin and Deloris grew up together more like brother and sister. Austin's goal is to become a police detective. He is six feet tall, has blonde hair, blue eyes, and a square jaw.

Timothy "Tim" O'Malley – A seasoned detective at the Kansas City Police Department where he has worked for thirty years.

~ DELORIS'S COWORKERS AT THE SWITCHBOARD ~

Beverly "Boo" – Deloris's co-worker.

Joyce – Deloris's co-worker.

Loreda "Lori" – Deloris's co-worker.

Mary Virginia Miles – Manager of the KCPD switchboard and Deloris's supervisor.

Pam – Deloris's co-worker.

~ THELMA'S BOARDERS ~

Annie Bailey – Has a quiet demeanor and loves finding out the story behind something. She is a pretty girl with a cute round face, a few freckles sprinkled across her nose, blue eyes and curly strawberry blonde hair that she wears short in an effort to control it. Annie works at the *Kansas City Post* newspaper.

Grace "Gracie" Burnett – A cool, calm, and collected young woman with long blonde hair, blue eyes and a warm, glowing personality. When everyone else panics, Gracie calms the waters. She takes classes at Kansas City Junior College. When not at school she works at the KCPD switchboard.

Leota Jones – A boarder at Thelma's boarding house with brown eyes and short, straight, mousy brown hair that she still wears in a 1920s pixie style. She works as a maid at the President Hotel and babysits Thelma's daughters while Thelma works.

~ THE SULLIVAN FAMILY ~

Mrs. Sullivan – Paul's mother. She married a travelling salesman who never returned from a trip out of town. She takes in laundry and cleans houses to support her children.

Mary Margaret Sullivan – Paul's twelve-year-old sister. Though only a child herself, she takes care of her younger brother and sister while Mrs. Sullivan works.

~ THE ADCOCK FAMILY ~

Marguerite Adcock – A childhood friend of Thelma's. She is a comely looking woman with a slender build who wears her long brown hair put up in a bun. She lives in an affluent neighborhood in Kansas City.

Harry J. Adcock – Marguerite's husband and vice president of the First National Bank. Stolid and serious, he appears older than his years.

Tommy Adcock – the eight-year-old son of Harry and Marguerite Adcock. He is a stout, active boy with short curly blonde locks and a cherub's face.

Prologue

THE INTRUDERS

A s Marguerite Adcock took a pan of bread rolls out of the oven, there was a knock at her front door. She quickly turned off the oven, stirred the soup she made for lunch, and then, wiping her hands on her apron, went to open the door. There stood an unfamiliar, nice-looking young man dressed in the electric company's uniform. She guessed he was about twenty-something.

"Yes?" she asked cautiously.

"Good afternoon, ma'am. I'm with the electric company and we had a report of some problems with the power lines in the area."

"We don't have any problems here," she replied, starting to close the door.

He stepped forward and put his foot in the door, blocking her attempt.

"Just the same ma'am. I need to check your fuse box to make sure it wasn't damaged in the last power surge. It fried some wires in other houses nearby."

"All right, but please do it quietly. My son is asleep upstairs."

"I will do my best," he said with a friendly smile.

Marguerite showed him to the basement door and told him that there was a pull string light at the bottom of the stairs.

"The fuse box is on the left," she yelled down to him before going upstairs to check on her eight-year-old son, Tommy, who was home from school with the chicken pox.

A few minutes later when she descended the stairs from her son's room, she saw the man was at the landing looking up.

"It looks like you have a fuse and a wire that are damaged and should be replaced. I need to go out to my truck to get replacements and I will come right back."

"Okay," Marguerite replied, slightly annoyed at the interference with her lunchtime preparation.

Less than five minutes later the man returned and barged into the house followed by another young man dressed in a mechanic's coveralls and a scruffy beard. They ran to the kitchen and the nice-looking man grabbed. She struggled in his arms and tried to scream, but he covered her mouth with his hand. When she bit him, he spun her around and slapped her hard. Then the scruffy looking man quickly stuffed a dish rag in her mouth, securing it with a tea towel tied around her face. Fighting for control, Marguerite clawed at the uniformed man who was still holding her and managed to scratch him on his arm, drawing blood.

The scruffy looking man then grabbed her hand and started taking her wedding ring off of her finger. Marguerite managed to wrestle her other arm free and scratched him on the neck. He loudly threatened to break her finger if she didn't stop resisting. With fear in her eyes, she complied as he wrenched the ring off and slipped it into his pocket.

When Tommy heard the scuffle and his mother's cut-off scream, he came running downstairs. Seeing the struggle, he came in with fists flying, biting and kicking at the men attacking his mother. Marguerite tried to take advantage of Tommy's attack but was unable to break away from the electric company guy's iron grip. While she struggled, Tommy bit the man in the coveralls on his arm and drew blood. Then the boy kicked him, and when the guy bent down to rub his shin, Tommy balled up his fist and got a good blow to the man's nose, almost knocking him off balance. Tommy pushed the man, trying to send him to the ground, but he recovered enough to punch Tommy in the stomach and send him doubled up to the floor.

Moving quickly, this man tied Tommy's hands behind his back and gagged him, while the electric company man tied his mother's hands similarly. Mother and son were led to the basement, where the intruders proceeded to tie ropes around their ankles and place them with their backs against a wall. The intruders turned off the light, plunging them into darkness, and ran up the stairs, bolting the basement door behind them. Tommy and Marguerite heard them going back and forth from room to room, their heavy footsteps causing the floor to creak from their weight. Hours later, there was the faint sound of the front door closing. Everything stayed quiet and Marguerite assumed they had gone.

Sitting in the dark, she tried to stay calm as she and Tommy worked to untie their hands. As they were fumbling with the ropes, the front door creaked open, causing both captives to stop and hold their breath. Upstairs, they could hear someone enter and walk across the floor. Moments later, Marguerite heard the comforting voice of her husband Harry calling their names. With gags still in place all they could make were muffled noises. Kicking about wildly in the darkness, Marguerite managed to hit a shovel with her feet. It ricocheted into a low shelf and sent a glass canning jar crashing to the floor.

Hearing the shattering glass, Harry unlocked the basement door, expecting to see the family's cat come flying up the stairs. When no cat appeared, he grabbed a rolling pin from the table and cautiously started down the stairs. As soon as he pulled the string to turn on the light, he spotted his wife's shoe next to the bottom step on the floor. As he descended the stairs he saw the shattered jar, and then his family to the right. Rushing over to them, he dropped the rolling pin and started untying mother and son.

"Are you hurt? What happened?" he asked as he untied them.

Free from their bondage, a crying Marguerite and Tommy hugged Harry so tightly that he couldn't move, but then he didn't want to move just yet. He was relieved to know they were okay.

Upon hearing their story once they were back in the kitchen, Harry called the police. While the family waited for the police to arrive, they looked around to see what was missing and what damage the intruders had done. The house had been turned upside down and several valuables were missing. The case of silverware that Harry's mother had given them for a wedding gift was missing, as were the silver candlesticks inherited from Marguerite's aunt—even the silver soup tureen with its matching ladle was gone.

Running upstairs to her bedroom, Marguerite found her silver hairbrush and comb set missing, and an empty space where her jewelry box had been. The jewelry box reminded her to look at her left hand where her wedding ring was absent. Feeling overwhelmed, she sat on the bed, fighting back tears.

Tommy burst into the room carrying his piggy bank. "Mama!" he said, a big grin on his face, "it's still here! All two dollars and forty-nine cents. They didn't take it!"

Marguerite gave a weak smile. "I'm so glad to hear that," she said. "But now you need to get back into bed. I need you to heal up from the chicken pox so that you can be big and strong and go back to school."

"But Mom," he said, "what if I need to protect you again? I was giving that burglar a good fight until he sucker punched me."

"The police will be here soon, Tommy. You were so brave this afternoon, but you need to get back in bed and rest now."

Dismayed, Tommy's shoulders drooped as he started to leave the room but he came back to his mother and hugged her. Then he said, "Hey Mama, I'm hungry. Can we eat now?"

"Oh, my goodness! You are right. We did miss lunch, didn't we? Please wash your face, change your pajamas, and climb back into bed. I'll bring you something to eat for supper."

Remembering the rolls from the oven and the chicken soup she'd left simmering on the stove hours ago, Marguerite hurried downstairs to the kitchen, afraid the soup had boiled dry. However, when she got to the kitchen, the stove was off, and only traces of soup remained in the pot. The freshly-baked rolls were gone too. All that remained of her lunch were some dirty bowls left on the counter, minus the silver spoons that the intruders must have taken after they'd finished eating.

"The dirty birds!" Marguerite exclaimed, which was the closest she'd ever come to cursing in her gently bred life.

"Marguerite?" Harry asked, slightly shocked.

"It's simply all too much, Harry." Marguerite had a cross between anger and despair upon her face.

"Once the police finish talking to us, I'm taking you to the hospital. I called the doctor and he says that you should get checked out." Harry took Marguerite's hand in his own and placed them both on her stomach. "I want to make sure that everything is alright with both you and the baby."

Marguerite nodded and put her other hand on top of Harry's as there was a knock at the front door. She turned toward the stove to fix something to eat and Harry went to answer the knock. He let the police in and they started asking him questions as he showed them around.

"Where were you this afternoon?" one of them asked a bit suspiciously.

"I was at work," Harry explained.

"Uh huh," one of the officers said as he wrote in his notebook.

Harry felt obliged to continue, "I work at a bank, but I didn't get home at my usual time because I had to wrap up a few things first."

The officer looked like he accepted Harry's statement and said, "Can you show us where the items were taken?" After going through the house, Harry and the officers entered the kitchen.

"Marguerite, the officers would like to ask you a few questions and then we need to go to the station to provide an official statement."

Marguerite nodded, stopped her preparations, and sat down. She gave them a description of each man, as best she could remember. No, she had never seen them before. No, she didn't see what vehicle they were driving. Marguerite felt that she wasn't much help because she only paid attention to the men when they started grabbing her and tying her up. "It all happened so fast," she bemoaned. "I need to find someone to stay with Tommy, then I'll be happy go to the station." she added.

As soon as the police officers left, Marguerite called her longtime friend Thelma Webb and relayed her horrifying afternoon. Thelma operated a boarding house and was busy with dinner for her boarders, but she promised to send someone she trusted over to watch Tommy.

CHAPTER 1

Going to the Big City

W hen Deloris graduated from high school on Thursday, May 7, 1931, she wanted to escape from small town Missouri life. She had one boy who proposed to her and another one who vowed his eternal undying love. Others tried to capture the elusive butterfly without success. While this was a lovely dilemma to have, she wanted to see more of the world before she tied herself down. Deloris admired the women who married farmers and worked side by side with their men, but she decided long ago that being a farmer's wife was not the life for her. She was always drawn to the big city from when she visited her big sister, Thelma.

Momma and Dad were both concerned about their little girl going to the big city, but they knew that once she had her mind made up it was a wasted effort to try to change it. At least Thelma was there if she ran into any problems, she convinced her parents. When her oldest brother, Roy, heard she was going to Kansas City, he wrote his friend David Kerns, who also lived there to keep an eye on her too. It wouldn't hurt to have someone else there in the city with her best interests in mind.

"Are you sure about this, DeDe?" Clarence asked. He was Deloris's second-oldest brother.

"Positive," Deloris replied.

"And you aren't afraid?"

Deloris stood as tall and proud as her five-foot two-inch frame could allow and shook her head. "Nope. Roy and Thelma left, didn't they?"

"Yeah, but they were both married," Clarence reasoned.

"Well, it's no longer the Victorian age, and women can do anything nowadays, even vote."

"I never said you couldn't vote, I just want to make sure you'll be safe."

Deloris looked up at him, "Haven't you ever wanted to see the world, Clarence?"

Clarence shrugged, "I've been to St. Louis and to Denver. People are people, I reckon, 'bout anywhere you go."

"Do you think I'm making a mistake?" Deloris watched her older brother's face intently.

Clarence smiled. "I think you need to live your own life, DeDe, wherever that takes you. Just remember you have family here and I'll always be around if you decide you need a ride back to Jameson and the farm."

At these words, Deloris hugged her brother tight.

"Here now," he protested, "you'll smush your corsage, and I don't want to be walkin' around smellin' like your fancy perfume."

Deloris rolled her eyes at her brother, adjusted her corsage, and said, "Maybe if you smelled a little sweeter, you could get a girlfriend."

"It isn't the way I smell, it's my face that they don't like."

Deloris shook her head at her brother. "It isn't your face, it's your brains they're concerned about," she replied, and then hastily turned tail and walked to her seat before Clarence could respond.

On the stage at graduation, Deloris sat down next to her classmate Alphia Thompson. Deloris was a year older than Alphia, but that didn't matter to them. They'd been friends since first grade. Deloris was a year older because she had to start first grade over after the Spanish Flu outbreak caused all schools in Missouri to cancel the entire school year. In fact, Deloris was a year older than most of her classmates. On Deloris's left was Irving Barton.

"Ready to graduate?" Irving asked.

"I can't wait to leave this one-horse town," Deloris answered.

"DeDe, Jameson has at least 200 horses, and that's not counting all of the farms between here and Pattonsburg," he laughed.

"Thank you for counting. I'm glad to see you didn't fail math class." Deloris gave Irving a stern look but he just continued laughing, oblivious to her sarcasm.

Alphia looked around and saw another classmate, Liam O'Casey, staring at Deloris.

"What did you do to Liam?" Alphia whispered in her ear. "He's been glaring at you since you arrived."

"I broke up with him last night," Deloris whispered back. "He told me not to go to Kansas City or he would break up with me so I told him to get lost."

"That would explain why those guys,"—Alphia pointed at two more of their classmates at the other end of the stage —"are both trying to catch your eye. Do you think all your potential beaus will have fisticuffs after the ceremony? Winner gets to date you?" Alphia laughed.

"I've got to get out of town before another one of them proposes," Deloris said. "I don't want to be a farmer's wife."

"What do you want to be?" Alphia questioned.

"I don't know, but I need to find out."

As Deloris finished speaking, the school superintendent walked to the front of the stage. He welcomed everyone to the graduation ceremony for the Jameson High School class of 1931. Deloris straightened the lavender gown that accented her violet eyes and waved at her friend Austin Martin in the audience, doing her best to look like a mature, responsible eighteen-year-old.

After the ceremony, Deloris and Alphia stepped down from the stage to find their families in the audience and Alphia continued their conversation.

"Are you serious about leaving town?"

"What's this about you leaving Jameson?" Austin came up behind them.

"What are you doing here? You graduated last year, remember?" Deloris commented.

"Oh, I had to come and see if you finally graduated," Austin teased.

Deloris stuck her tongue out at him.

"So, did I hear correctly? You are leaving town? Where are you going?" Austin persisted.

"Kansas City. My sister Thelma has a room open at her boarding house. She said I could stay there as long as I get a job and pay her rent. Clarence was supposed to take me this weekend, but his car broke down. He had to order a part for it and the hardware store isn't sure when it will arrive." Deloris looked at Austin. "Will your mother be at home this afternoon? I'd like to use her phone to call Thelma and let her know I won't make it."

"Instead of calling, I could give you a lift. I'm headed down Sunday if you want to ride with me?" Austin said.

"Yes!" Deloris said eagerly, but then hesitated. "The thing is, would you promise not to fall in love with me?"

Austin grinned, "DeDe, I know you far too well to fall in love. Go flutter your eyelashes and give someone else the glad eye, someone who doesn't know that you're a vixen and stubborn hellion."

The classmates partied all weekend. They celebrated at each other's homes on Friday then on Saturday they partied on the banks of Big Creek, where the cold, spring rain left everything a muddy mess. One classmate wore her dad's overalls to protect her clothes and another hitched up an old dress to make it pants like and dove into the mud. Deloris wore her boots and an old long coat, but with slippery footing and mud fights, everyone was a mess when they went home.

After a weekend of partying, Deloris packed and prepared ready for her big adventure. On Sunday afternoon, Austin pulled up to the Markham farmhouse. Dad went over to shake Austin's hand and inspect the tires on his car to make sure they were up for the trip to Kansas City. Once Dad had deemed the car road-worthy, he helped Clarence and Austin load all of Deloris's luggage, trunk, and boxes.

Momma looked at her daughter, "Don't forget to give Thelma the cornflake cookies I made and don't forget your manners, neither. You best help your sister with cleanin' up the place, as well."

"I will, Momma," Deloris promised.

"I expect you to be in church every Sunday and don't you be running 'round with strange men. Don't get yourself in those situations."

As Momma finished giving her instructions, the men came back to the porch. Deloris gave big hugs to her family and pretended not to notice when Momma wiped away a tear. She got into the car and waved goodbye until they crossed the creek at the bottom of the hill and she couldn't see the farmhouse anymore.

Once they were on 13 Highway, away from Jameson and almost to 6 Highway, Deloris turned to Austin. "In all the hubbub after graduation, I never asked; how is your police training going?"

"Well, I graduated from the Police Academy six months ago and I also took some additional classes at the Kansas City Junior College. As you know, they consider the high school diploma from Jameson equivalent to two years at a junior college so I only had to take a few extra classes and I was done. I guess you could say that everything is hunky dory."

"So, you're a police officer? I didn't realize that you were finished with your training and already qualify as a police officer. Which police force?" Deloris asked.

"Kansas City, Missouri Police Department," Austin said with a sense of pride.

"Don't you have a relative who is a police officer?"

"Yes, I have a cousin who is a captain with the North Kansas City Police Department. He wrote me a letter of recommendation for the Police Academy and set up an interview with his department for me, but I didn't think it would be good for me to work directly under him. I applied and was accepted with the KCPD. I've been working there for almost a year."

"You're a police officer," Deloris repeated to solidify it in her mind. "I can't believe it."

"I hope to be a detective one day," Austin said.

"Oh, you'll be a detective! Easy peasy."

"Not quite so easy, DeDe. The first year on the force is probationary. That started when I went to the police academy after I graduated from Jameson last year. Once I'm off probation, I can potentially become a junior detective, and then after another year, I can apply to be a full detective. But in order to be a full detective, you need a recommendation from a current detective and that can be hard to get. I've already applied for a junior detective position, and I'll find out if I get that position as soon as I'm done with my probationary period."

"So, you're almost a detective."

"Not quite. This is more like a trial period. They can decide I'm not qualified to continue at any time."

"You've got nothing to worry about, Austin. I remember playing cops and robbers with you when we were in grade school. You always wanted to be the cop, so I had to be the robber."

"DeDe, you couldn't even play a pretend cop. You never follow the rules."

"Oh, so I'm a robber?"

Austin laughed, "Not a robber necessarily, but definitely not a police officer."

Deloris laughed too and continued, "Where do you live?"

"I have an apartment not far from the station, but currently I am staying at a local hotel. One of the units in my building caught fire and even though I don't have fire damage, there was some smoke and water damage to my apartment. The fire department won't clear us to go back until repairs are made."

"I see. If you don't want to stay in a hotel, when we get to Kansas City I can talk to Thelma and see if you could stay at her boarding house for a week or so, until your apartment is ready," Deloris offered. "She can't rent you a room, though, her boarding house is all-female."

"If she agrees, I might take her up on it for a few days. It would sure help me out," Austin smiled. "Until I can either move back into my apartment or find another place."

"Stay at Thelma's," Deloris urged. "Save your money."

"If you're sure she won't mind."

"Nope, my sister's got a great big heart, she won't mind."

CHAPTER 2

Thelma Webb

As Austin's car purred down the highway towards Kansas City, Deloris looked out of the window at the rolling hills and thought about her sister. Thelma did have a big heart, but she didn't have it easy and the current economic depression made the situation worse. Thelma was short and round with long red hair that she wore braided and put up in a bun. Married and divorced twice with two daughters in tow, Thelma worked two jobs and took in boarders just to keep a roof over their heads. She never got help from either of her ex-husbands. The boarding house she bought with help from the girls' grandparents.

The girls' father and Thelma's first husband, Claude Webb, was a fly boy in World War I. When he came home to his wife in Coffey, Missouri, after the war, Thelma became pregnant right away and gave birth to her first daughter. Soon after, she found herself pregnant again with a second baby and gave birth to her second daughter eleven months later. Having seen Paris and London, Claude felt trapped and found country living too boring. He headed to

California to seek his fortune, leaving a pregnant Thelma and a young daughter behind.

Deloris had overheard Thelma telling their brother Roy's wife, Bert, that when Claude landed in New York after the war, he met a woman. They stayed in touch through secret letters and the woman convinced Claude to join her in California. Thelma filed for a divorce based upon his desertion and won. Funny thing, Thelma heard from Claude's mother that he didn't find a fortune in California, he was stuck pumping gas there—a not-so-glamorous job. His parents were so embarrassed that their only living child did this to his wife and their grandchildren that they helped Thelma buy the boarding house to help her support herself and the girls. They disowned their son and gave Thelma what would have been his inheritance, and since they were fairly well-to-do, it was a large sum that allowed Thelma to buy a larger house to set up as a boarding house.

Thelma met her second husband, Walter McKinley, when she first came to the city. He was a real smooth talker who wooed her and courted her like she had never been treated before. He probably thought that she had a lot of money to own such a big house, but he was wrong. He convinced her that he was going to hit it big one of these days. She soon learned what "hit it big" meant to Walter.

Eventually Thelma discovered that Walter had a penchant for trouble when he was arrested one month after they were married for attempting to rob a bank.

Walter claimed that he was forced to commit the crime and told the story this way: "I told the officers that I was just standing there waiting my turn at the teller cage, when three gangsters came in with guns a-blazing to rob the bank. I didn't want the other people in the bank to get hurt, so I told all of them to do as the robbers said. Then I stood to one side to let the robbers finish their task. I was concerned for everyone's safety and was just trying to help the robbers along so that nobody got hurt. But the other people in the bank told the police that I was one of the bank robbers and the police believed them, so I was arrested."

Because it was his first offense and they couldn't prove he was one of the robbers, Walter was only sentenced to six months in jail as a possible accessory. Thelma believed him on the bank robbery and shared his story with Deloris when she asked Thelma what was wrong.

Within a month of getting out of jail, Walter immediately got into trouble again and was arrested for a train robbery. This time he was sentenced to two years in jail. An inmate he met while serving his six months in jail had talked him into a quick and easy heist. The guy knew of a place where the railroads stored their fully loaded box cars until they hooked them up to a train. Unfortunately, they forgot to have someone act as a lookout and the security guard caught them in the act with an armful of merchandise and more goods in their car. A second security guard called the police and both were arrested. The other fellow was shot when he tried to run.

Walter explained to Thelma that he was only trying to find a package on the train that hadn't been delivered to him yet. The package was an anniversary present for Thelma, in fact, which was why it was so important for him to try and get it directly from the boxcar because it was going to be late. The security guard just didn't listen when he tried to explain this to him. Thelma was skeptical, but Walter being the smooth talker he was, won her over again. Deloris overheard the two of them arguing about that when she was there babysitting. His smooth talking also swayed the judge, and he only got a short two-year sentence. When Walter was released from jail, he returned to Thelma, but wasn't long before he was in trouble again.

Deloris read all about Walter's last escapade: robbing another bank. The newspaper headlines told about a bank customer walking across the street who observed four individuals exiting two motor cars carrying Tommy guns and entering the bank. Two more gangsters sat in the cars with the motors running, ready for the getaway.

The customer ducked into a nearby store instead and told them to call the police. As they were calling, one of the robbers shot the security guard who fell at the bank entrance, bleeding. When the police arrived, they arrested the two drivers in the getaway cars and then waited outside with guns drawn to ambush the robbers. Two robbers were shot so Walter and the other robber put their guns down in surrender. Walter gave state's evidence on his accomplices and received a reduced sentence. Thelma heard one excuse after another from Walter and he still managed to talk himself back into her life. That is, until he messed with her family. That was the straw that broke the camel's back.

Walter considered himself a ladies' man and continually stared at Deloris when she stayed with him and Thelma. One day, it turned physical and he got fresh with Deloris, who was distraught by his advances. When Thelma found out she filed for an annulment and said – "bye-bye" to Walter McKinley. Deloris accompanied her sister to the court for the ruling. Afterwards, Thelma reclaimed her first husband's last name, Webb, so she would have the same name as her daughters.

Coming back to present-day thoughts, Deloris started imagining this next chapter in her life. Thelma's boarding house originally had one bedroom and the only bathroom on the first floor. The second floor had three bedrooms and she had another bathroom added, the third floor had the nursery suite where her daughters slept, another bedroom, and a bathroom. On the fourth floor was a large open attic space filled with broken furniture, trunks, boxes and whatever else Thelma needed to store. The main bedroom downstairs was Thelma's, and she had the carpenter who lived next door convert the screened in back porch into a bedroom so that she could take in another boarder. When all of the rooms were full, Thelma could house five boarders, but right now she only had three. When Deloris stayed the previous summer, she slept in the smallest bedroom on the third floor next to the nursery. Thelma told Deloris that she could have a room on the second floor now since she would be paying rent. She liked the rooms on the second floor the best because she would have a bit more privacy. Still, Deloris thought, as the skyline of Kansas City came into view, shimmering a bit in the late afternoon sun, any room would do, because none of them were in her parents' home. She smiled and Austin caught the movement.

"Ready for Kansas City, DeDe?"

The smile became a grin, and Deloris replied, "Is Kansas City ready for me?"

CHAPTER 3

The New Boarder

W hen Deloris and Austin arrived at Thelma's boarding house, they found the front door unlocked so they entered carrying two of Momma's boxes of food. The boarding house was quiet. Deloris found a note from Thelma in the kitchen, propped up against a rhubarb pie, that said that Thelma and the girls went to the park to play and would be back in an hour. it went on to say that the pie was for Deloris and Clarence to eat after she moved in and that the bedroom Deloris would be staying in was on the second floor at the end of the hall.

Deloris looked at Austin, grinned, and said, "Clarence isn't here so I guess this is your lucky day. I think we need to eat the pie first, to give us energy for the move-in."

As she was cutting two pieces, Deloris heard a meow and turned to look behind her. A gray cat walked toward her.

"Oh no!" Deloris cried out, already starting to feel her nose tingling. "*Achoo!*"

As Deloris started sneezing, a door opened above and there was a clatter on the stairs. A young lady with curly, strawberry blonde hair cut short stuck her head into the kitchen.

"Is everything all right?" she asked.

"—the cat—" Deloris managed to get out between sneezes, "— I'm allergic, *achoo*!"

The strawberry blonde scooped up the cat and carried it away. Austin opened the kitchen window and Deloris started to feel better.

The young lady entered the kitchen again. "The cat is back in Leota's room. She's only supposed to let it out when no one's home."

"Thank you!" said Deloris.

"I'm Annie, by the way. You must be Deloris. I moved in last fall, right after you left. I've heard lots about you from Thelma. And who is this?"

"Hi, I'm Austin. A friend of the family."

"Hello friend. Thelma told us you were coming, Deloris. Would you like help moving into your room? I've got the bedroom at the end of the hall next to the bathroom and yours is on the other side, second on the left."

"Sure. Oh, and you can call me DeDe. All of my friends do. I've seen all the rooms before when I stayed with Thelma last summer, but I do want to see mine and decide if I need to move anything around."

Annie and Deloris carried two of her bags to the bedroom while Austin went to the car to get the rest of Deloris's luggage and her trunk. He then carried the luggage up to the second floor, and Deloris helped with the trunk.

"What have you got in this thing, rocks?" Austin asked as they lifted the trunk up each stair. "When did you decide to move the entire town of Jameson to Kansas City in all of these bags? Do you have the bandstand from the park in the trunk?"

Huffing and puffing, he made one comment after another until Deloris retorted, "Two of the bags contain gifts for Thelma and my nieces from Momma. The two boxes we left downstairs have vegetables, eggs, fresh milk, a fryer chicken, and so on, also for Thelma. So, none of those things should count as mine. The trunk has some books in it."

Two big suitcases, a trunk, three boxes, and two bags later, Deloris was moved in. At that moment, Thelma walked in, followed by her two girls. When the girls saw Deloris, they ran to hug her. After greeting her nieces, Deloris asked Thelma if Austin could stay with them until his apartment was declared livable by the fire department or he found a new place.

"Fire? Austin, you need a place to stay?" Thelma asked slightly surprised.

"Yes, ma'am."

"I'm not a ma'am to you. I'm Thelma, remember?"

"Yes, ma'am. I mean, Thelma. That's just my police academy training kicking in. Sorry," Austin replied with a smile.

"I do have an empty room. You can stay there until you can move back to your apartment or find another."

"Thank you, ma—Thelma," he caught himself.

As Austin went out the door for the last time to retrieve his one bag, another boarder walked in the door.

Deloris introduced herself and the boarder mumbled, not looking Deloris in the eye, "I'm Leota, I have the room on the third floor next to the nursery."

"She's the one with the cat," Annie interjected.

Leota glared at Annie and quickly turned to head upstairs.

"Is she always like that?" Deloris asked.

"Pretty much," Annie replied.

Once Austin returned with his bag, Annie showed him the other empty bedroom on the second floor that was to be his room.

"This is temporary, right?" she asked. "My parents would flip if they knew there was a man staying in my boarding house."

"Just for a few nights, I promise," Austin said. "I'll start looking for a new place tomorrow just in case my old apartment was too badly damaged by the smoke and will require a major remodel."

Deloris and Annie hit it off very well. They talked and giggled as they unpacked Deloris's bags, and Annie said that it was as if they'd known each other for years. When Austin came downstairs, he found them eating more pie in the kitchen.

"Hey, save me some," he complained as he walked over and got another piece for himself.

"All right you three, you need to save some room for supper," Thelma cautioned.

"But it is so good," Deloris retorted.

Thelma, smiling, shook her head and started to raid what was left in the food boxes that her momma sent to make a quick dinner. Annie and Deloris helped her put things away and Deloris remembered to set out the corn-flake cookies for after dinner.

As they finished unpacking the food, Deloris glanced out the kitchen window and spotted a woman in her fifties pulling her car into the garage behind Thelma's house. The woman entered the house through the back door and walked into the kitchen.

"Hello," Deloris said. "I'm the new boarder, I have one of the bedrooms on the second floor and this is Austin. He is only going to be staying with us for a short time."

"I thought this was a female-only boarding house," the woman said, looking at Thelma with concern.

"Yes, ma'am," Austin quickly replied. "It's only until my apartment can be repaired after a fire in the building or I find another one."

"It wasn't your apartment that caught fire, was it?"

"Oh no. It was an apartment two floors above me and across the hall."

"Good. As long as you don't start a fire here or make a lot of noise, we'll get along fine. My name is Wanda," she replied with a smile. "Nice to meet you. I have a recipe for a special laundry soap to help get the smoke smell out of your clothes, if you need it."

"Wanda, would you like some dinner?" Annie offered.

"I'll just take some bread and cheese back to my room," Wanda said. Once she'd gotten her food, she exited the kitchen through the back door, closing it quietly behind her.

Deloris looked at Annie, "She seems nice, but a little blunt."

Annie smiled, "She's usually fairly cordial. Sometimes she comes home very tired. Something must be bothering her today. She probably just came home from visiting her son, Terry. He has a live-in girlfriend and Wanda *hates* her. She's in a better mood during the week. She works as a teller at a bank and is only home in the evenings. Something must have happened at Terry's."

"Why did she go out the back door?" Austin asked suspiciously.

"Oh, that's another room now," Thelma responded. "I

had Ben Davis from next door wall in the back porch to add another room to rent. Wanda was living in the bedroom Deloris will move into, but when I converted the porch into another room, she asked if she could move into it. She thought it would be quieter and away from the cat. She is allergic to cats, too." She looked at Deloris and nodded.

"I like her already," Deloris said.

"Here is your key to the front door," Thelma added as she handed Deloris and Austin each a key. "Be sure to lock everything up if you are the last one out of the house. A few months back, Wanda and I came home at the same time and found Walter lurking around inside when no one was home."

"Not a problem for me. I don't want him in the house even when you are here," Deloris responded.

Austin had a concerned look on his face and Deloris explained, "Walter McKinley is Thelma's ex-husband."

After dinner, Thelma took a quick nap before going to work. In the living room, Leota read a romance novel, the girls played with the paper dolls that their grandmother had sent them, and Annie read a magazine. Across the hall, Deloris and Austin split the want ads from the Sunday newspaper, spreading them across the dining room table. Austin focused on the apartments-to-let, going through the listings in a methodical fashion. It must be lovely, Deloris thought a bit enviously, as she watched him, to have such a clear plan for life. She wished she knew what she should be doing. Her goal had been to get away from Jameson and she'd accomplished that, but now what?

Austin circled another apartment listing as Thelma got

up from her nap and took her daughters upstairs to the nursery to put them to bed. Deloris remembered her promise, that she'd find a job and pay rent for her room. Thelma couldn't afford to have her stay there for free. Deloris realized that her next goal was to find a job, any job. Otherwise, she'd have to go back home.

Deloris didn't want to be another burden on her sister, and she definitely didn't want to return to Jameson, so she turned back to flipping through the want ads. However, all of the openings that caught her eye required experience, which she didn't have.

Thelma came into the kitchen after putting the girls to bed just as Deloris said, "Harrumph!" and tossed the newspaper onto the table, scowling at it.

"No luck?" Thelma asked. Deloris shook her head.

"There'll be another paper tomorrow," Austin said encouragingly.

"How about the egg factory?" Thelma asked. "I could introduce you to the hiring supervisor. It doesn't pay very well, but they're usually hiring."

"That's awfully sweet of you," Deloris said, though the egg factory didn't really sound like very much fun. Still, she told herself, it would be a job.

"My shift is from ten o'clock at night to six o'clock in the morning," Thelma said. "I'm getting ready to leave now, but before I go, I'll write you directions on what streetcars to take to get to the factory. You can meet me at the front gate at ten after six, and I'll take you in."

As Thelma left the kitchen, Deloris saw that Austin was smiling broadly from the other side of the table. "What?" she demanded.

"If you work in an egg factory, I think you're guaranteed to get egg on your face," Austin said.

"Hush!" Deloris said.

"Ain't nobody here but us chickens," Austin chortled, and then retreated to his bedroom before Deloris attempted to put an egg on his face.

CHAPTER 4
The Egg Factory

Monday morning, as Deloris arrived at the egg factory, she looked up at the large two-story warehouse that had been painted white and took an apprehensive breath. So, this is where Thelma spends her nights, she thought to herself. She walked through the gate and saw Thelma waiting for her at the entrance to the building. The two of them walked into the factory and Thelma guided her to the elevator. Once inside, Deloris asked Thelma to tell her about the job.

"There's not much to the work. Don't volunteer to do cleaning, that's the most... odorful part of the job. You want to stay on one of the lines. They will probably start you out as a packer. As long as your crates are packed with minimal breakage by the time the drivers need to load them onto their trucks for deliveries, you'll do fine. Once there's an opening, you can move into grading, where you put the eggs through a device that sorts them by their weight. I prefer weighing and grading and I think you will too."

"How many shifts are there?"

"Three. There's the morning-to-afternoon, afternoon-to-evening, and overnight shifts. I like the overnight shift on Sunday night to Thursday night. It pays an extra five cents, plus I get home in time to fix the girls breakfast, take a nap, and then go to my other job at the lunch counter. This way, I can see my daughters in the morning and in the evening. I also have my Fridays and Saturdays free. Leota watches the girls for me during the day, when I go to work at the lunch counter and when I take naps, plus she stays with them overnight. It helps her to pay her rent, because she doesn't make much money working part-time in the mornings at the hotel. When the girls are in school, she only has them overnight. That's when she takes more shifts at the hotel."

Deloris looked around the front office area. While it was calm here, she could hear the bustle of people at work and smell the unmistakable odor of chicken manure. It wasn't overpowering, but it was definitely there.

Thelma knocked on a door and the sisters were invited to enter. As they did, Thelma explained that she was checking to see if there were any jobs available and the hiring manager, Mr. Campbell, smiled. Someone had just quit that day. Deloris was hired, if she could start tomorrow, covering the hole in the afternoon shift. They shook hands and Deloris promised to be back on Tuesday at one-thirty, so she could be shown her duties before her shift began at two.

"This is probably everyone's favorite part of the factory" he stated. As they walked outside of his office, he pointed to the time clock that hung on the wall and showed her where to get a punch card from the stack on the desk below. He indicated the line to write her name and how to operate the machine.

"Try to check in about five minutes early. There are

lockers in the restrooms on the first floor for you to put your personal belongings in."

"Yes, sir."

"Are you ready for a quick tour of the factory?" Mr. Campbell asked as he stood up from his desk.

"Yes, sir," Deloris replied, eager to get started.

Smiling, Mr. Campbell turned and headed down the stairs toward the back of the facility with Deloris and Thelma following him.

Thelma stopped and slyly said, "I'll wait for you here. I've seen that part."

Deloris and Mr. Campbell walked to the back of the facility through the big double doors that were kept open in the warm weather for ventilation. Outside, Deloris saw another long building. At the far end was a large noisy motor with two belts moving around and around on each side of the motor.

Opening the door to this building, Mr. Campbell waved his arm for Deloris to enter. Suddenly, she felt a tingling of her nose from the pungent smell of ammonia. Quickly grabbing a handkerchief from her purse, Deloris held it up to her nose and walked over to two long rows of cages stacked four high. Each cage had one hen inside.

"Sorry about the smell," Mr. Campbell apologized. "We have those two big fans in here to help with cross-ventilation, but they can't keep up. That is why we clean this area once a week and add fresh bedding. Unfortunately, that doesn't happen until tomorrow morning."

"I'll manage," Deloris responded.

Mr. Campbell proudly explained about the new conveyor system that they saw outside, just installed last year.

"The motor with the two belts is used to operate this

two-track conveyor system." He pointed to one of the tracks that ran in front of the row of cages. Another track ran on the opposite side.

Deloris and Mr. Campbell then went back in to the front part of the factory where they met up with Thelma.

"How was it?" Thelma whispered to Deloris.

"Breathtaking."

"I know," Thelma laughed. Mr. Campbell grinned and they continued to the egg-cleaning side of the factory.

Deloris saw a batch of eggs being hosed down, wiped down, and dried. The dried eggs were placed in layered egg trays that were stacked three high and placed on a cart. The cart was rolled over to the next stage where the workers determined the size of the egg with a measuring tool. Afterward, the eggs were placed on a scale and weighed.

Mr. Campbell explained that consumers were very concerned about the size and weight of the eggs and wanted to be certain that they weren't being cheated. "Based upon the size and weight, they are placed in separate trays that are marked small, medium, large, extra-large, and rejects. The rejected eggs are damaged somewhere in the process or have some abnormality in size or shape. Employees are welcome to take the rejects home for their use. I think Thelma has taken advantage of that offer a few times. Am I correct, Thelma?"

"Yes, I have, and I am very grateful for the opportunity to have them."

Mr. Campbell continued, "The trays are carted over to a table where those women remove each egg, place it in an egg carton, and mark the carton with the size. They pack the cartons into wooden boxes that are loaded on trucks for transport."

"I see." Deloris was a little overwhelmed with all of the

processes, but she knew that she would get it all down as time progressed. This was a far different experience with eggs than Deloris had ever experienced. Back home, she just went to the hen house, pushed the old hen off the nest or reached under her to gather up the warm eggs and put them in a basket. Momma said that they shouldn't be washed until we were ready to use them because they would last longer. She never imagined such an operation like this existed.

"Well, what do you think?" Mr. Campbell queried.

"It looks like a very well-organized system to me. In which part of the factory will I be working?"

"The opening you will fill is in packing. You will pack the crates and prepare them for loading on the trucks. Is that okay with you? I can check into switching you around, if you prefer another area."

"Oh no, that is fine with me. Thank you, Mr. Campbell. I'll see you tomorrow."

As she rode with Thelma on the streetcar taking them back home, Deloris shook her head. "I never thought I'd be working with chickens again after I left the farm."

The sisters laughed at the irony as they watched the streetcar come upon a large queue of men standing on the sidewalk. The men were quiet and gaunt, almost all of them looking at the ground. They didn't even bother to look up when the streetcar passed.

"The egg factory isn't a glamorous job, but it is a job," Thelma said. "After my last divorce, even with the house, I didn't know how I was going to keep a roof over our heads and feed the girls. My friend Marguerite knew the general manager of the factory and she recommended he hire me."

"I know, a job's a job, especially in these times," Deloris said as the streetcar finally drew even with the start of the long line of men, who were waiting to enter a soup kitchen. "And I'm glad you've got a friend like that."

Thelma nodded. "I might have bad luck with romance, but I've had good luck with my friends."

The streetcar arrived at the sisters' stop, where Thelma and Deloris exited and started walking towards home.

"How is Marguerite doing these days?" Deloris asked. "I haven't talked to her since the last Jameson picnic."

Thelma smiled. "She's doing well. Harry, her husband, treats her like a princess and Tommy is a cheerful bundle of rambunctiousness."

"How did Marguerite know the egg factory manager?"

"It was through Harry. He works at the First National Bank, where the egg factory keeps its accounts. I guess the manager and his wife became friends with Harry and Marguerite."

Deloris and Thelma arrived home just as Leota and Wanda were leaving. Leota headed to her job at the hotel, and Wanda told them that she had an early staff meeting. Annie was just getting up, and Austin was in the kitchen, filling the percolator with water and coffee grounds. "How'd it go?" he asked. "You look like the cat that ate the canary. Or should that be the cat that ate the egg?"

Deloris groaned. "Your jokes are so bad, they're painful."

"I guess it's a good thing I'm not a comedian, or you'd be throwing rotten eggs at me."

Thelma shook her head at the two of them and started making breakfast.

"I got a job. I start tomorrow afternoon."

"That's great news, DeDe!" Austin replied. "Everything is falling into place for both of us."

"What fell into place for you?"

"I called the manager this morning and found out that my apartment will be ready to move back in by Friday— earlier than I thought. It had minimal damage and not much smoke. Just like I told them at the time," Austin said smugly.

"That's great news, too!" Deloris said. "We should celebrate."

"We could celebrate over breakfast," Austin replied, "Maybe with scrambled eggs?"

Deloris threw a dish towel at Austin. He caught the towel, grinned, and went to get a mug for his coffee.

"Deloris, could you stir the eggs," Thelma asked, "while I finish frying the bacon and take the biscuits out of the oven?"

"Anyone want coffee?" Austin asked.

"I'll have some orange juice," said Thelma. "I'm going to take a nap once I see the girls off to school."

"I'll squeeze the orange juice for you and everyone else once the eggs are done," Deloris offered.

When everything was finished cooking, Thelma and Austin carried the food into the dining room while Deloris juiced the oranges. Thelma headed up to the third floor to bring her daughters down and Austin started setting the table. With a smile, Deloris got a stepladder to reach Thelma's best cut-glass coupe glasses that had been a wedding gift from her first marriage. She carefully poured orange juice into six of the fancy glasses and another two glasses of milk for the girls.

She'd just carried the glasses into the dining room when she heard a clatter on the stairs as Annie, Thelma, and the girls all came down.

"Those are some ritzy orange juices," Austin commented.

"We're celebrating, remember," Deloris chortled. "I

have a new job and you, and your terrible sense of humor, are leaving." Austin started laughing.

"What's this?" Annie asked.

"I can move back into my apartment on Friday," Austin explained, "but I promise I'll still come around to provide some egg-cellent jokes."

Deloris was happy for Austin that he could move back to his apartment Friday, but it was a little disconcerting that one of the only two people in Kansas City she knew well was moving out of the boarding house so she wouldn't see him as often.

Austin saw her face, and said, "Don't worry, DeDe, I'll still be around to annoy you. Just behave, so I don't have to arrest you for anything."

After breakfast, Deloris offered to handle clean-up as Thelma took her daughters to school and Annie and Austin left for their jobs. Once the dishes were done, Deloris took the trash out the back door, when she saw a young man hanging around what had been the back porch door but was now the door to Wanda's bedroom.

"May I help you?" she asked.

"Oh, uh. I was just waiting for my mom."

"Oh, you must be Wanda's son. She's already left for work today. I'm Deloris, another boarder."

"Yeah, uh, I'm Terry."

"Nice to meet you," Deloris started to say, but Terry turned and walked off quickly. Strange young man, she thought to herself.

CHAPTER 5

The Leeds Lunch Counter

W hen Austin arrived home after work, Deloris was sitting in a chair in the living room, tapping her nails and staring fixedly at the phone. Annie was in the dining room, cutting articles out of an old newspaper and jotting down some notes.

Deloris entered the dining room, and Annie, looking up from her project, asked, "Everything okay, DeDe?"

"I'm not sure. Thelma called and had Leota pick up the girls from school. That was hours ago. The girls and Leota are upstairs, but I don't know where Thelma is."

Austin checked his wristwatch. "When does she usually get off work? It's almost six o'clock."

"She should be home by..." Deloris didn't finish her statement because just then, the front door opened and Thelma walked in.

"What's going on with you?" Deloris queried. "You're never late."

"I know," Thelma agreed. "The lunch counter was robbed today, and I had to stay to give the police a statement."

"Oh no!" Deloris exclaimed. "Are you all right?" She hurried to Thelma's side to comfort her.

"I'm fine. Just a little shaken up," she replied.

"What happened?" Austin asked. "I've been out on a case and didn't go back into the station."

"How did this happen?" Deloris asked.

"Don't the police eat there? Weren't any of them there when it happened?" Annie questioned, entering the living room.

"Hold on," Thelma said. "Let me catch my breath."

Deloris led Thelma into the kitchen and sat her down at the table. Austin served up a piece of pie, and Annie put on the kettle. After taking a bite of pie, Thelma began to tell the story.

"Yes, the police are typically in getting coffee, or they come in for lunch because the station is only a block away. The crooks must have been watching because as soon as the last policeman left, they came barging in. They told the cashier to give them all the money out of the cash register. That was thirty dollars. Then they told me and the other cook to stand aside while they pulled the safe out of the corner of the kitchen."

"Oh my gosh, Thelma! I am so glad that you're okay," Annie said.

Thelma continued, "I guess there was about seventy dollars in the safe and thirty in the cash register. I heard our boss say that to the police. They also took my boss's silver stick pin that was valued at about ten dollars. All in all, they got away with about one hundred and ten dollars."

"Oh Thelma," Deloris said. "Did they take anything of yours?"

"No, but I only had a few coins in my purse and you know I don't wear jewelry."

"Lucky for you that you are poor, huh?" Deloris said with a soft, sympathetic smile. Thelma sighed, then smiled wearily.

"Thelma?" Annie asked. "Would you be willing to talk to a reporter?"

Seeing the confused look on Deloris's face, Annie explained, "Oh, I didn't get to tell you. I work for the *Kansas City Post* newspaper. I have been just a gofer, but today I was promoted to the crime beat reporter's assistant. I know he would be very interested in interviewing someone who was there."

Thelma looked torn. "Momma always says that a lady should only have her name in the paper when she is born, when she is married, and when she is deceased."

"Momma," Deloris replied, "doesn't understand the modern world. Mrs. Lou Hoover makes regular radio broadcasts and has lots of newspaper stories written about her. She's President Hoover's wife, you know. You can't say she's not a lady."

"That's true," said Thelma, wavering. "But it's late. Would he still be there?"

"Reporters work all hours," was Annie's reply.

"Plus," Deloris continued, "it would help out Annie."

"I might even get a chance to help write the story if I bring in an eyewitness account," Annie said.

"It might also help the police," Austin pointed out. "If you describe the robbers in the paper, someone might recognize them."

Austin's argument won the day. Thelma relented and agreed to talk to the reporter, then went upstairs to check on her daughters.

Annie ran to the phone to call the crime reporter and came back a short time later. "He wants to interview you,

Thelma, and I checked," Annie said, "he agreed to quote you as Mrs. X so you don't even have to have your name in the paper if you don't want. We can go right now to do it, so that you can come back and catch a little sleep."

"I guess that's okay, then. Leota can watch the girls."

At that, Annie whisked Thelma away to the newspaper office for her interview.

"Well, I had better go talk to the apartment manager about moving back into my apartment," Austin said as he got up from the table.

"Aren't you going to stay for supper? My cooking isn't that bad," Deloris said disappointedly.

"I guess I can wait until after supper."

"So, where exactly is your apartment anyway?" Deloris asked as she served them both a meatloaf. "All you said before was that it was close to the police station."

"It's next door to the farmer's market, not too far away from here, so I can still keep an eye on you and everyone here."

"You think you're supposed to keep an eye on me? What gave you that impression?"

"Um—" Austin stumbled for words.

"This wouldn't be something Clarence or Roy put you up to, would it?"

"It's just... you're one-hundred pounds soaking wet."

"Uh-huh," Deloris tapped her foot. "And you think I can't handle things?"

"If I had a baby sister running amuck in the big city, I'd be a little concerned, too."

"Let me tell you a story, Austin. And this is a secret only a few people know."

"Okay?" Austin said cautiously.

"I'm halfway responsible for my sister's second divorce."

"Is that supposed to reassure me?"

"Hush," Deloris took a deep breath. "What do you know about Thelma?"

"Not too much. She's what, fifteen years older than you?"

"Eleven years older. Thelma left school when she was fourteen. Anyway, she's been married twice and, as I said, it is partly my fault that her last marriage broke up. Last summer I came to Kansas City to help Thelma with the girls. One day, Thelma asked her husband Walter to drive me to my cousin's house in Raytown for a birthday party. Once we were in the car alone, he put his hand on my knee and started going up my leg. I threw his hand off but he tried it again, getting rougher. So, I took off my shoe and hit him in the head with the heel. You know, the heel on my shoe is solid wood and if I ever need to protect my virtue, I just take it off. It makes a mighty fine weapon."

"Deloris—" Austin started, but Deloris kept going.

"There's more to the story, though. When I hit him, it caused him to run the car off the road and hit a tree. When he swerved the car, it spun me around and I hit my back on the dash of the car when it hit the tree. Because I was facing him when I hit him, I was thrown into the dashboard. I whacked my back pretty hard, but I was in better shape than Walter. He was barely conscious, slumped over the steering wheel and groaning. He was bleeding from his mouth and the hole in his head from the heel of my shoe," Deloris grimaced faintly and paused. She looked directly at Austin. "When I tell you I can handle things, it's the truth. I almost killed him."

"Thank goodness you didn't. Did you tell Thelma?" Austin asked.

"I got out of the car and started walking to my cousin's

house. A pickup truck stopped and gave me a lift. Once I got to my cousin's, I called Thelma and told her everything. The next day, Thelma was at the lawyer's filing for another divorce, and I was at the doctor's, having my back looked at."

"I'm sorry for your sister," Austin said.

"Thelma just isn't very good at picking men."

"But you're good at hitting them with your shoe?" Austin asked.

"Exactly!" Deloris said with a gleam in her eye.

Thelma returned home about an hour later from the newspaper, happy but exhausted since she'd barely slept all day.

"How did your interview go?" Deloris asked.

Thelma's eyes danced, "Oh DeDe, it was so much fun. I got to go into the newspaper building and they treated me like a celebrity or something. Annie showed me the printing press. It's three stories high! Then the reporter asked me all about what happened. It'll get published in the paper tomorrow and they're calling me Mrs. T."

Deloris had never seen her sister so animated before. She usually was more reserved and serious. Deloris promised that she'd run out and buy a passel of newspapers early the next morning so Thelma could mail the article to all her friends. Thelma thanked her and went to take a short nap before she left for her shift at the egg factory.

Deloris stayed up to wait for Annie, who was still at the newspaper, assisting the crime beat reporter finish the '*Leeds Lunch Counter Looted!*' story so it could make it into the morning paper. When Annie finally arrived home, she was so excited she could barely sit still.

"They let me write part of it," she exclaimed to Deloris. "Not much of it, but I wrote up the description of what the lunch counter looked like. Imagine that, my words are going to be read by all of Kansas City tomorrow!"

CHAPTER 6

Pals and Buffoons

Deloris and Annie didn't get to sleep until after midnight, but that didn't stop Annie from knocking on Deloris's door early the next morning. Deloris was only half awake, but the two girls hurried out to the corner newsstand. They got there just as a *Post* delivery truck rumbled past. The truck slowed down and a man in the truck bed tossed out a bundle of newspapers before it picked up speed and continued down the street.

Deloris and Annie ran to the bundle. They heard a "Hey!" behind them. The newsstand proprietor stood there looking stern. "You gonna buy those papers?" he asked.

"Yes, sir," said Annie. "We'll take fifteen copies. Our friend was interviewed yesterday because she witnessed a crime."

The proprietor was happy to make such a big sale and he quickly cut the twine holding the bundle. "That'll be thirty cents," he said, and Deloris handed over three dimes.

When they got back to the house a few minutes later, Austin was making coffee in the kitchen. Deloris took fourteen copies to Thelma's bedroom and set them on her dresser while Annie spread the other copy on the kitchen table and turned to the crime section. The three pals read the story together. Most of it they already knew, but the reporter had asked Thelma what the robbers looked like. Thelma hadn't seen their faces because both of them wrapped handkerchiefs around their faces and pulled their hats down low. She did notice that two of the robbers were wearing expensively tailored suits, while the third one wasn't. The crime reporter had shown Thelma pictures of suits and ascertained that the two robbers wore English Drape suits, which were very fashionable and quite expensive.

"I hope they catch them," Annie said.

Deloris looked at Austin, "Maybe you'll track them down."

"I appreciate your belief in me," Austin said. "But I am a police officer, not a detective, yet. Plus, I haven't been assigned to this case."

"How long did you say it'll take for you to be a detective?" Deloris asked.

"I need to be assigned to shadow a detective and assist with his cases first. I've requested it, but I'm still waiting to hear if that will happen. After a period of time if the detective recommends me and it is approved, I will be promoted to detective. But that typically won't happen for a while."

Austin finished his coffee and grabbed his uniform jacket and hat. "I've got to be going so I'm not late for work. Unlike some people, I have to work mornings." He gave Deloris a wink and she rolled her eyes. He quickly left before she could give any retort to his comment.

Deloris poured herself a cup of coffee and sat down at the table with Annie.

"Do a lot of people work at the egg factory?" Annie asked looking up from reading the paper.

"Scads," said Deloris. "Why?"

Annie laid the paper down and said, "I don't think Thelma has had any luck finding someone to move in here from the night shift. Could you see if any of them from your shift are looking for a room? Now that Austin is moving out, it would help Thelma to have another boarder."

"Good idea. I'll ask around," Deloris said.

"Just be sure that whoever you find isn't whacky. They'll be living across the hall from both of us."

"I'll be careful," Deloris promised.

"Thanks," said Annie. "And now I've got to run. The crime reporter who interviewed Thelma said I could come along with him today to assist with another story."

That afternoon, as Deloris stood in her bedroom, she made a face in the mirror. Her dark hair was in an elegant updo, but her coiffure didn't match her dress. She'd put on an older dress she had worn to do chores on the farm and she sighed as she looked at her reflection. Fashionable it was not, but the chickens wouldn't care.

Deloris arrived at the egg factory thirty minutes before her shift. She clocked in, grabbed a white apron, and went to Mr. Campbell's office. He showed her where she would be working and introduced her to her shift supervisor.

"Deloris, this is C.J. Marwood."

Her supervisor was a young man about twenty-five years old, and more convinced of his attractiveness to the fairer sex than was warranted. When he saw Deloris, he smiled.

49

"Hey, Girlie."

"Hello, Mr. Marwood," Deloris said, as politely as she could.

"Call me C.J., all my friends do," he said.

"I'm not sure we're friends yet," Deloris replied. "We've only just met."

"Well, I believe we will be good friends," he said with a sly smile. "You see, my father owns this here facility and I like to be very friendly with all the fillies who work here, especially dollfaces like you. I noticed you right off."

"If I'm going to work here, Mr. Marwood, I need to go do my job," Deloris said, and hurried past him to her place near the packing crates.

The rest of her first day was uneventful. Packing eggs into crates wasn't the glamorous future she'd hoped to find in Kansas City, but it meant she'd kept her bargain with Thelma and she could officially become a boarder. When the whistle blew at ten that evening, she was ready to leave. As she walked out of the factory, she met Thelma walking in.

"How was your first day?" Thelma asked.

"It was fine," Deloris said, not wanting to bother Thelma by telling her about C.J.'s behavior. "Boring, but fine."

The following afternoon, as Deloris was walking to the packing area at the back of the egg factory to start her shift, she heard a wolf whistle behind her and C.J. Marwood sauntered up.

"Hello there, cutie patootie. What's shaking besides your curves?" he asked.

Deloris almost told him to scram, but she managed to hold her tongue. One of the girls glared at her as she walked by. Deloris heard that the girl imagined herself to be C.J.'s girlfriend.

Over the next few days in the factory, Marwood became a constant pest. He fancied himself a Casanova and flirted with all the women who worked there. While the women did their best to avoid him, Deloris quickly learned that none of the other supervisors or managers would ever discipline or report him because his father was the boss.

After a week of his overly 'friendly' behavior, Marwood started asking her out. At first, Deloris managed to either have an excuse when he asked or avoided his advances altogether by hiding behind the egg trucks when she saw him making his way toward the packing area. Deloris didn't want to worry her sister, so she decided not to tell Thelma what was going on. Marwood was only around during the day, so Thelma never had to deal with him.

One day, when she was trying to get an extra-large order of eggs packed and ready to go, she missed his approach. As he walked behind Deloris, he pinched and groped her behind. She spun around and slapped him hard across the face, leaving a red mark. She didn't intend to hit him that hard, but what was done, was done. He stood there stunned for a minute, holding his jaw, and then said,

"You're out of here! Grab your stuff, clock out and go."

Deloris turned to leave and then spun back around to face him.

"You should be ashamed of the way you treat the girls in this factory," she said, loud enough that half the factory could hear. "Does your mother know you're nothing but a sleazy, no-good buffoon?"

At that comment she turned so sharply that her skirt

flared up slightly. The girls on the assembly line started to clap but stopped when he looked around and glared at them. They didn't want to lose their jobs, too, but looking down the line, all but one had a smile upon her face.

Deloris stopped at that girl's workstation and said, "You want him? You can have him. I never wanted him in the first place." She stormed out, slamming the door behind her.

Luckily Thelma and Deloris had different last names and worked different shifts; otherwise, Marwood probably would have fired Thelma, too, just for spite. Thelma's shift supervisor liked her, though, and he and the hiring manager never told anyone that she was Deloris's sister or that she had recommended Deloris for the job.

After she'd been fired, Deloris went straight home. As soon as she walked in the door, Thelma heard her and got up from her nap. She wanted to know why Deloris was home so early. Deloris told her what happened and Thelma became as angry as a wet hen. She started out the door to give Mr. Marwood a good tongue lashing, but Deloris managed to talk her out of it. Thelma was better at sticking up for others than sticking up for herself. She was generally meek and mild, but if someone messed with her family, she could declare war on them in an instant, just like she did with Walter.

Deloris got Thelma to sit and calm down. She didn't want to be responsible for Thelma losing her job too. Coming to her senses, Thelma shook her head and said, "Men like that are just no good."

"You are correct, they are not," Deloris agreed, "but I

can find another job. I bought a newspaper on the way home, surely there'll be some place I can work." Thelma didn't look convinced, but Deloris insisted, "You go back to sleep, and I'll get something started for supper. I will check the classified ads after dinner."

Once supper was over and Thelma had gone to work, Deloris grabbed the newspaper and started perusing the want ads. She wasn't interested in being a butcher's assistant and she'd never learned to drive, so she couldn't deliver coal or ice blocks. As for being a maid, she could do it, but cleaning was not something she excelled at or enjoyed. Plus, Leota was a maid and she didn't even make enough to pay Thelma full rent.

Halfway down the paper, a small ad caught her eye. Poppy's Paradise Park was looking to hire a soda jerk. The pay looked good, but Deloris had never worked a soda fountain before. How hard could it be? she thought. She watched the pharmacists in the neighboring towns of Pattonsburg and Gallatin scoop up ice cream and put it in cones. Sometimes she ordered a milk shake and saw them make that too. It didn't seem that hard. Convinced she could do it, she circled the ad.

The next morning, she was in the kitchen waiting for Thelma to return from her overnight shift at the egg factory. When she came in, Deloris offered her a cup of chamomile tea and showed her the Poppy's Paradise Park ad.

"The amusement park? Do you know how to soda jerk?" Thelma asked, surprised.

"Well, no, but I bet that I can pick it up pretty quickly. It doesn't look that hard," Deloris said with as much confidence as she could muster, trying to convince herself in the process too.

With a skeptical look upon her face, Thelma stared at Deloris for a moment, and then shook her head as she turned to go to her bedroom for a few hours' sleep before she left for the lunch counter. Deloris grabbed a pencil and paper and went to the phone to call Poppy's Paradise Park and set up an interview.

CHAPTER 7

Poppy's Paradise Park

Deloris caught the bus to Poppy's Paradise Park the next morning. She found the business office in a six-room building at the back of the park. The front office was bright and cheery-looking, and Deloris felt that she would really like working here. She interviewed with a Mr. O'Brien, who had a smile that lit up his friendly face. She told him that she wanted to apply for the soda jerk position and he asked her if she had ever done that kind of work before. She lied, putting on her most convincing, confident face again. He hired her and told her to start that weekend. Mr. O'Brien told her that her shifts would be Friday, Saturday, and Sunday evenings, the busiest hours of the park. She would work with the other weekend soda fountain employee for an hour, and then be on her own until the park closed.

Leaving Mr. O'Brien's office, she stopped a moment to take in the smell of freshly popped popcorn. To the left she saw a concession stand that advertised popcorn, cotton candy, and snow cones. The girl who was salting the popcorn looked up and smiled.

From there Deloris decided to check out the soda fountain so she wasn't walking in unfamiliar on her first day. When she opened the door to the soda fountain, a small bell that hung over the door jangled alerting the girl behind the counter that someone had entered. Startled from not expecting anyone to come into the soda fountain before opening hours, she looked up from her cleaning and asked, "May I help you?"

"Oh, my name is Deloris and I'm just here looking around. I will start working here Friday."

"Look all you want," she said as she continued wiping down the counter.

Deloris stood there for a moment to scan the room before walking around. There were two ceiling fans moving in unison to help keep the place cool and the floor had small mosaic tiles that alternated black and white. In the front were four round wooden tables with white wrought iron legs, each with four wood and white wrought iron soda parlor chairs with red leather seat cushions. Placed in front of the eight-foot-long counter with its red and white Formica design were five stools with red leather seats. Two booths painted white with red bench seats stood on each side of the soda fountain counter. In the corner on the left sat a jukebox that was playing a Cab Calloway song, filling the air with his crooning about "Minnie the Moocher."

Deloris ventured a step behind the service counter to get a better look. The back wall had three large mirrors and a work area countertop. The register was in the middle with glasses on the left and sundae dishes and silverware on the right. A large chalkboard sign hung over the mirror in the middle advertising the different delicacies served at the fountain. At the far end of the counter against the closed-off side was the carbonated beverage dispenser, which included some of her favorite soda pops, like Polly's Pop and Coke. Next to that was the mixer for malts and other blended ice cream treats. On the customer service counter were the syrup dispensers and a variety of toppings from chopped nuts to cherries and strawberries. In the middle of the counter was the open freezer stocked with all the best ice cream flavors. Various tools like ice cream scoopers and mixing spoons hung at its side.

Satisfied that she had a grasp at least of where things were if not of what the job would require, she went shopping for some comfortable shoes since she would be on her feet all evening long.

When Friday came, she checked in at the office to sign her paperwork and was told she'd be paid by check every Friday. Then she went next door, through the break room and to the left, to the women's dressing room and lockers. The men's lockers and dressing rooms were on the right. Mr. O'Brien told her that she would find the uniform that she was required to wear in the dressing room. Two girls were already in the dressing room when Deloris got there. One girl was in a stall changing into her uniform and the other one was holding a swimsuit.

"Hi, my name is Stella. You must be new here," the one with the swimsuit said.

"I am. My name is Deloris. Mr. O'Brien told me to come here to get my uniform and change," Deloris replied. "Today is my first day; well, actually this evening."

"Nice to meet you. Trudie is in there," pointing at the dressing stall.

Through the curtain, Deloris heard, "Hi there. Really my name is Gertrude, but you can call me Trudie." She poked her head out of the modesty curtain that covered the changing room. "I work at one of the concessions stands selling popcorn and cotton candy." Trudie emerged from the dressing room. Smoothing her apron down, she continued, "Stella here is a lifeguard at the Crystal Pool." Holding her hand out to shake Deloris's hand, she said, "Pleased to make your acquaintance."

"Where are you working?" asked Stella.

"I'm at the soda fountain."

"Oh, you'll be working with Paul Sullivan," Trudie said.

"Is that good?"

"He's okay. Nice looking, but quiet and a little shy," Trudie added. "He's friends with Mr. O'Brien, so watch what you say around him."

"I'll keep that in mind."

"You need to clock in over here," Stella directed her to a wall with a clock and timecards. "Put your name on one of the blank cards and put it here to punch the time on it. You're a little early for your shift, aren't you?"

"I wasn't sure how long it would take to get checked in and ready," Deloris said.

She'd also hoped that if she got to the soda fountain early, she could spend that time watching Paul and learning how to soda jerk, she thought to herself.

"Makes sense," Stella said. "We're early because the bus can run late, so we take an earlier bus. Mr. O'Brien doesn't like tardiness."

The uniforms are in here," Trudie offered as she showed Deloris the attached room where she saw several white dresses in various sizes hanging on a rod.

"Thank you both for your help."

"No problem, honey. Oh, and just pick a locker to put your purse and things in," Stella added. "Any locker that still has the key in the lock is empty." Stella then stepped into the stall to change.

Looking through the dresses until she found her size, Deloris pulled one out from the group. By the time she found a dress, Stella was finished changing and stepped out of the stall so Deloris stepped in and put the dress on.

When she stepped out, Stella smiled. "The aprons are here next to the dresses." She opened a large cupboard where red and white striped aprons were neatly stacked inside.

"And you'll need a cap," Trudie added, as she grabbed two matching garrison-style caps from a stack on a shelf above the aprons. She handed one to Deloris and put the other one on her head.

"Thanks again," Deloris said.

The white dress made the red and white striped apron, topped off with the red and white striped garrison cap, stand out. Deloris found an empty locker and put her purse and clothes in it. She locked it and put the key in her apron pocket. Taking a final glance in the mirror, she decided that she looked like a walking, talking peppermint candy, but it was still better than how she looked at the egg factory.

Deloris hurried over to the soda fountain twenty minutes before her shift started. That should give her enough time to meet this Paul Sullivan, have him show her where everything was, and figure out how to get started.

At the soda fountain, she found Paul easily. He bashfully introduced himself and told her he had worked at Poppy's Paradise Park as a soda jerk for about five years. She guessed that he was about thirty-five years old. He was tall with a slender build and had thinning, sandy colored hair. Paul was terribly shy and hardly looked Deloris in the face. When he did, he quickly looked down.

Deloris tried to pull him out of his shell, but once the introductions were made, Paul left before the hour was up and she was on her own. He didn't provide any instructions, just a "See ya tomorrow." Deloris was annoyed that Paul had skipped out on his shift early, but she didn't want to rat him out to the boss and make an enemy of him on the first day, remembering what Trudie told her about his close friendship with Mr. O'Brien.

In came her first customers, a family of three. They all ordered an ice cream cone, two chocolate and one vanilla. The ice cream scoop was easy to find and the cones were simple enough to do. Okay, that went well, she thought as she gave a sigh of relief. Next was a mother and son, who also ordered ice cream cones.

Behind them was a young couple. She ordered a chocolate milkshake and he only wanted a Coke. Okay, here goes, Deloris thought as she put three scoops of vanilla ice cream in the mixer along with some milk and a healthy amount of chocolate syrup. She turned on the mixer and watched to see when the ice cream was blended with the chocolate. Then she poured the rich chocolate mixture into a soda glass and put a straw in it. As she handed the young woman the drink, the woman asked, "Where is the extra syrup on the top?"

"Oh sorry," Deloris said as she squeezed the syrup on the top. "This is my first day." The Coke was easy to pour. The couple sat in a booth in the back talking for a while, and then finally went on their way.

Nothing more difficult than that first milkshake happened for the rest of the day. She went home elated that she had succeeded in doing a job that she had absolutely no experience in.

The next day, Paul stayed to the end of his shift and showed Deloris where a few things were. Apparently, it pained him to talk to her because he left as soon as he could.

It was a rainy Saturday, and the soda fountain was empty until Deloris's first customer walked in. He was a handsome man in his late twenties, who ordered a strawberry sundae.

"Yes, sir. Coming right up," she said. Then she turned to grab a glass to put it in.

"Don't you intend to get one of those oblong dishes?" he said pointing at a stack of small dishes that could hold two or three scoops of ice cream.

"Oh yes. Silly me," she said with a smile.

Deloris put the glass back and took one of the dishes and put two scoops of ice cream in it. Under the counter she saw something marked strawberry syrup so she poured that on top and handed it to the man.

He looked at it for a minute and then leaned over the counter and whispered, "You don't really know what you are doing, do you?"

Whispering back, she said, "I don't, but I really need this job."

Standing back, she watched him think for a minute. Then he grinned and walked behind the counter where he pointed to a container of chopped strawberries.

"First, you use real strawberries on a strawberry sundae, as well as syrup." The man took the dish Deloris had handed him and sprinkled the chopped strawberries on top of it. "The syrup normally goes on top of the strawberries. Then you top it with whipped cream and put a maraschino cherry on top."

"Thank you," Deloris replied sweetly.

"Now, pretty lady, would you like me to make you a strawberry sundae?" the man offered.

"Unfortunately, I'm allergic to strawberries," Deloris confessed. "I'm not sure how I'll make strawberry sundaes if I have to touch the strawberries."

"You can always use gloves and a spoon and be cautious when pouring the syrup." The man winked and said, "I'd also recommend you not eat them. How about I make you a Black and White? Or would you like a Traffic Light Sundae or Missouri River Ale?"

Deloris smiled, "I don't think I'd better, sir, since I don't know what any of those are and I don't even know your name."

"Miss, er uh, I don't know your name either," he smiled back leaning on the counter. "My name is Leon Iraklidis, and if you'd like, I can stop by tomorrow evening to teach you a little more."

"That'd be swell," she said, as she reached out her hand to shake his. "Deloris Markham. I'll be at work tomorrow evening and I'd love some help. Where did you learn all of this?"

"I was a soda jerk in Chicago. Now I install and repair soda fountain equipment."

"I'll be sure to call you if the equipment stops working," Deloris promised.

"Can't call me if you don't have my number," Leon said with a wink. He pulled out a notebook, jotted down his phone number, and passed a sheet of paper to Deloris, who modestly smiled and tucked it in her pocket.

With Leon's help that night and the following night, Deloris learned how to be a soda jerk. She could understand customers who told her to "Make it Cackle" (whip in an egg), "Paint it Red" (add cherry flavor), or "Draw Some Mud" (serve up a coffee).

Just before closing on Sunday evening, Deloris finished the last drink Leon said she needed to learn, a Catawba Flip. First, she mixed vanilla ice cream, a fresh egg, grape juice, and shaved ice in a blender. Once the mixture turned into a smooth purple cream, she put it into a glass, and gently folded in seltzer water and vanilla ice cream so that purple and white swirls could be seen through the sides of the glass. She topped the ice cream soda with whipping cream and grape syrup, tucked in a long-handled spoon, and handed it to Leon.

Leon made a show of inspecting the drink before taking a sip. "First-rate!" he said. "But did you know this drink goes by another name, one that might be more fitting for Kansas City?"

"What's that?"

"Well, Kansas City is a big cow town, right? You've got the stockyards and the American Royal Livestock Show."

"What does that have to do with an ice cream soda?"

"The other name for a Catawba Flip is a Purple Cow."

Deloris laughed, "You're right, that is a better name for a Kansas City ice cream soda."

Leon smiled, started to say something and then hesitated.

"Go ahead, spit it out," Deloris said. "Oh, not the drink," she laughed. "What did you want to say?"

"I'll be out of town for the next two weeks; I'm headed to Wichita for an installation and then Joplin for a repair. I sure would like it if I could give you a ring when I get back. We could catch a flick and I could tell you that you're an Eighty-Seven and a Half."

Deloris smiled. "It's a date, so long as you tell me what an Eighty-Seven and a Half means."

Leon winked, "In soda jerk lingo, an eighty-seven is a beautiful dame and the extra half means that she's got gorgeous gams."

Deloris laughed, scribbled the number to Thelma's boarding house on a scrap of a label from a bottle and handed it to Leon, who kissed it, and said "Hot diggity!" He tucked it carefully into his wallet and left with a wave.

When Deloris left Poppy's Paradise Park after closing up the soda fountain that Sunday, she was confident making sundaes, banana splits and all the other ice cream delights on the menu. Thankfully, Paul Sullivan and Mr. O'Brien were none the wiser. Paul continued to leave early and Mr. O'Brien hadn't come into the shop. They never saw Leon giving her lessons.

CHAPTER 8
The Regulars

Deloris's next weekend at Poppy's Paradise Park started just like the first: on Friday night Paul left early, leaving Deloris alone in the soda fountain. The soda fountain was packed with customers, and Paul's desertion was more frustrating than usual. As she hurriedly rang up orders, served drinks, and cleared tables, she started thinking about ratting Paul out when Mr. O'Brien walked in the door.

"Mr. O'Brien?" Deloris gasped in surprise as her boss came around behind the counter.

"I'm here to fill in for Paul," he said with a smile, putting on the red and white striped apron he'd been carrying.

"I wasn't expecting you to cover for him."

"I used to manage a soda fountain before I started working here," he explained. "Paul had to leave to take care of his family and he told me you were swamped with customers."

Maybe Paul wasn't as irresponsible as she thought. Deloris worked side-by-side with her boss for over an hour making sweet treats until the crowds slowed down. When it was finally quiet, Mr. O'Brien poured himself a root beer and told Deloris to get herself a soda.

"I'm impressed," he said, "you're great with people and you know your way around the counter. There's only one issue I saw."

Deloris tensed up. Was her secret out?

"I need to get you a stepladder for the back room," Mr. O'Brien continued. "I don't want you standing on crates to reach the top shelf. Can't have my employee hurting herself just because she's a little on the short side."

Deloris laughed and thanked her lucky stars that she'd had lessons from Leon. "A stepladder would be nice," she agreed, "but what happened with Paul? I didn't know he was married. Is everything okay with his family?"

"Oh, he's not married. He's only twenty-one, but he supports his mother and younger siblings," Mr. O'Brien explained. "His mother works, but she's not in great health. She was feeling poorly tonight, so Paul took off to take care of her."

"I didn't know," Deloris said. "I hope she gets to feeling better."

"I do as well."

"Can't Paul's father help out?" Deloris asked.

Mr. O'Brien shook his head, "No. His father is my cousin, and he was a good-for-nothing before he left his wife; I doubt he'll ever return. I found Paul a job here because I know he's trying to support his mother, a brother and two sisters."

"Thank you for telling me—I was a little annoyed at Paul when he left tonight."

"That's why I explained it to you, but please don't let Paul know that I told you all of this," Mr. O'Brien said. "I'm going to take off now, but I'll bring a stepladder by tomorrow. And before I forget, here's your paycheck. I'll leave Paul's in the office."

~

On Saturday when Deloris came into work, Paul and two guys who looked like mobsters were sitting at the front table in deep conversation. Paul called her over to the table as she came in the door.

"Deloris, there's a stepladder in the back room for you," he said.

"Thanks," she replied.

"Wonder what dollface did to get the boss to be sweet to her?" one of the strangers scoffed.

"Deloris, these are my buddies. This is George Nelson, but everyone calls him Brown."

George spoke up and added, "And this is my brother, Gordon, but we call him Babyface."

"Hey, don't call me that in front of the skirt," Gordon protested and hit him on the shoulder.

"Why not?" George turned to Deloris and continued, "We call him that because his face is as smooth as a baby's butt and he can't grow a beard because he isn't a man yet."

At that, Gordon jumped up and took a swing at George, who dodged his fist. Then Gordon landed a punch and George started to reciprocate. Paul stood up and wedged himself between the brothers, saying, "Hey guys, no fist fights in here. I don't want to pay for the damages."

Coming to their senses, the two men each adjusted their ties and straightened their suit jackets, snarling at each other.

Paul continued, "Bring us three coffees, Deloris, and be quick about it."

"Fine," Deloris said with a grimace as she walked back to the counter shaking her head. What a nerve he had giving her an order, she thought. She reminded herself that he was related to the boss and she didn't want to lose this job quicker than she had the last.

Deloris noticed that George and Gordon's presence at the front table scared other customers away from the soda fountain, making for a quiet evening. Customers would come in, see Gordon glaring at them, then order ice cream cones that they could take with them instead of staying to eat. There was something about how he looked, like he was itching for a fight and could attack at any slight movement, Deloris thought. That was probably why no one wanted to risk being around him, so the customers were leaving quickly.

As Deloris went to the back room to get a box of the wafers used in the cookies and cream sundae, she was grateful for the stepladder. It certainly was easier than balancing on one of the wooden crates that held extra bottles of flavorings. While she was standing on the ladder, she heard the bell over the door ding, and when she walked back to the counter, a customer carrying a brief-case was standing there. Paul was still at the table with George and Gordon, so Deloris asked the man what he'd like.

"A cherry phosphate, please," he said as he sat down at the counter.

Deloris got started, mixing cherry syrup and a bit of acid phosphate together in a tall glass. "What brings you to Poppy's?" she asked, nodding at the briefcase.

"Just finished a long day going door-to-door in this

neighborhood, saw the Park and thought I'd relax for a bit before heading home," he said.

"A traveling salesman?" she asked as she filled the glass with carbonated water, stirred, and handed it to her customer.

"Yes ma'am," he replied. He took a sip of the cherry phosphate, smiled, and said, "Do you have a life insurance policy? You know, you are never too young to need one."

"I'm sorry, sir, but I don't have enough money to purchase one right now. I just started working here."

"That's no problem. I can break it down into small monthly payments."

"Thank you, but all my money is spoken for and I don't want to get one at this time. Maybe later."

The salesman kept trying to sell a policy to Deloris. He was a little pushy and that bothered her, so she walked away from the counter using the excuse of cleaning the tables, even though they didn't need it. A few minutes later the man finished his drink and left.

Shortly after the salesman left, George and Gordon left as well, but she was surprised to see that Paul didn't go with them. Instead, he brought the coffee cups back to the counter and washed them.

Since the soda fountain was now empty of customers, Deloris opened a bag of roasted peanuts and started grinding them up into small pieces that could be sprinkled on ice cream as a topping. Paul lounged behind the counter and watched her work.

"How are you doing?" she asked. "You weren't at work yesterday."

"Oh, my mother was sick and I had to run some errands for her."

"How is she today?"

"She is doing better," Paul said. "We think it was just a little food poisoning."

Paul seemed to be in a friendly mood, and since he was hanging around without his friends, Deloris decided to ask him more questions about himself and his two buddies.

Paul told her that he lived with his mother, a younger brother and two sisters. His father was a traveling salesman and was seldom home. Then one day he never returned from a trip out of town. He just disappeared. At that statement, Paul started shaking his head and looking down at the floor.

"I've talked too much," he said suddenly, grabbing his cap and apron from under the counter where he had obviously stashed them earlier.

"No, don't stop. I want to hear about your father."

"I don't like to talk about him," he protested.

"Okay, how about your mother?"

Paul's face lit up at the thought of his mother and he relaxed, taking a seat at the fountain. "She is a saint," he said. "She holds our family together. She takes in other people's laundry and cleans houses, anything to bring money in to keep a roof over our heads. I give her half my paycheck to help out. One of my sisters is twelve now and started babysitting our younger sister and brother. It gives my mother more time to work outside the house cleaning other people's houses."

"Then why did you cut out of here early? You could get fired for that, you know."

"My mother was sick last night," Paul protested.

"And what about last weekend?

"Until I get caught, why not? It's a lot more fun hanging with Brown and Babyface."

"And when you get caught?" Deloris persisted.

"If I get caught, then I'll plead my case. Old Man O'Brien is related to my father and I think he feels sorry for me since my father left. It's easier to ask forgiveness than permission, you know."

"No, I don't know," Deloris replied, exasperated. "So, what about George and Gordon? That's their names, right? What's their story?"

"Yeah, well, they lost their father, too, when we were in elementary school. George was in my grade; Gordon is a year younger."

"So, you were all school chums?"

Paul nodded. "For a while anyway. When Gordon was in seventh grade, he got into a fight. That's where he got the scar on his cheek. He dropped out of school the next day because the other kid was put in the hospital in serious condition and Gordon knew he was headed to 'Juvi,' Juvenile Detention Center," he added when Deloris looked perplexed. "Anyway, before he could be taken there he cut out and they never caught him."

"So, Gordon never finished school?"

"Neither did George. I finished, but worked here while I was in school. I needed to help support my family."

"What do George and Gordon do?" Deloris asked.

"They've got several business ventures and I help them out occasionally," Paul said with a cocky grin. "Pretty soon, when a couple things come through, I can work for them full-time and leave this joint."

Holding hands, a young couple came into the soda fountain. Paul glanced at the clock and said, "Gotta go. I'm meeting them for dinner at the 12th Street Club," and then he slipped out the back.

As Deloris made a large banana split for the teenage couple to share, she thought about what Paul had said. It made more sense to her now why Paul was friends with George and Gordon, though she still wanted to know more about the "business ventures" the brothers were involved in. From the looks of them, she couldn't imagine an honest venture where they could make that much money to support the expensive clothes and fancy cars she'd seen them in. Her suspicions were awakened and she thought it wouldn't hurt to ask Austin to investigate. It might even help him get a promotion if the brothers were into something illegal.

What also surprised her was that Paul was only a few years older than she was. She would have sworn he was ten years older. He really needed someone to help him dress and look more age appropriate, she thought to herself. His clothes hung on him like an old man's, and his hat, a green tweed flat cap, had been crushed so many times it had become a flat shapeless blob.

CHAPTER 9

Paul's Friends

On her way home that evening, Deloris reflected upon what Paul told her about his friends. When she arrived home, she found that Thelma was still up. Even though it was one of her nights off from the egg factory, Thelma always kept the same sleep schedule.

"How are things going at the soda fountain?" Thelma asked.

"Good," Deloris replied, "but that reminds me" —Deloris opened up her handbag and dug out two bills— "here's my May rent. Fifteen dollars, right? Sorry it's a little late, I forgot."

"That's okay." Thelma said, taking the money. "It's not like I can't call Momma and complain if you don't pay."

Deloris laughed. "Anything but that! She'd have me moved back home so quick."

"Thank you for the rent. It really helps. Maybe the girls and I will get an ice cream cone tomorrow."

Suddenly, Austin knocked on the door, still in his uniform, and asked if he could come in. Even though it was late, they welcomed him. He took a seat on the sofa in the living room, looking exhausted.

"How's it going?" Deloris asked him. "You're working late on a Saturday."

"People are interesting," Austin said. "It is amazing what they try to get away with and how convincingly they lie. So far today, we arrested a pickpocket and a suspected robber. We broke up a domestic quarrel between a husband and wife and provided backup to another unit responding to a suspected mob hit. I just got done writing my reports."

"How many weekends do you work?"

"It varies week to week, but I'm working all weekend this week."

"That's so cool!" Deloris said.

"What about you?" Austin inquired. "How is the egg factory going?"

Deloris gave him the low down on what had happened at the egg factory and her new job at Poppy's Paradise Park, inviting him to drop by.

"That sounds like a sweet job," Austin stated. "You can sher-bet I will swing by."

Deloris groaned, and said, "I'll only let you in the soda fountain if you promise to never make a pun that bad again."

Deloris paused for a moment, and then told Austin all about George and Gordon Nelson and the almost-fight at the soda fountain. "I can't prove it, but I wouldn't be surprised if those 'business ventures' were fishy. Could you look them up in the police records? I want to know what they are up to, coming into the soda fountain."

Back at Poppy's the next day, Paul left early but seemed more at ease around Deloris when he said goodbye. Stella and Trudie dropped by on their break and after they left, Deloris fell into her routine of making drinks and sodas for the customers. She was now completely confident in her ability to make whatever ice cream treat a customer would request, and she'd started to get to know the regulars. In addition to the Saturday night couple that always shared a banana split, there were two teen girls who came by on Sundays and ordered ice cream floats, trying out every flavor combination they could concoct. Rocco and Rossi, Stella's cousins who worked at the nearby Indiana Gardens restaurant, would usually swing by during the lull between lunch and dinner on Sundays to order egg creams.

Rocco and Rossi had just left and Deloris was cleaning when Austin entered the soda fountain a few minutes before closing time.

"DeDe, have a minute?" Austin asked looking a little concerned.

"Sure, until another customer comes in. What's new?"

"I looked up those brothers, George and Gordon Nelson and their aliases, Brown and Babyface Nelson."

Deloris looked at Austin's face. "You found something, didn't you?"

"They have a rap sheet a half-mile long."

"Huh. I mean, I figured they were up to no good, but really, how bad is it?"

"The first thing I found were the records from their custody trial. The brothers' father was arrested for murder when they were ten and twelve years old. Someone made a note that their mother took to drinking, often leaving the brothers to fend for themselves. Eventually, the boys were sent to live with their grandparents, where their grandfather often beat them for any little thing, calling them demons. That came from an interview with the boys at the time. Their father died in a prison riot and their mother was found dead in the street one year later. The last entry in that record is a note stating that both boys had run away from home and couldn't be found."

Wow," Deloris said. "That is such a sad story. It must have been hard on George and Gordon to lose both of their parents in such tragic ways."

"Undoubtedly," Austin replied, "but that doesn't mean they're not responsible for their actions now."

"What actions?"

"In their late teens and early twenties it was small stuff, mostly pickpocketing, that led into pulling off a Kansas City Shuffle or two. Now they are suspected of knocking off a jewelry store and maybe even robbing a bank or two. They've been arrested for drunk and disorderly and had several trips to the drunk tank to dry out, plus a short stint in jail for beating up a police officer."

"Both of them?"

"Yeah, where one goes, the other follows," Austin paused, and then looked Deloris sternly in the eyes. "They're mean drunks, DeDe. Gordon almost killed a woman in a drunken rage. He'd have been locked up for a good long time, but she refused to testify at the trial, scared that Gordon's friends would finish the job if she did."

Deloris nodded, "Thanks, Austin. I suspected they were no good."

"I don't like them hanging around here. I looked up Paul Sullivan, too, but he doesn't have a record."

"Well, that's a relief. Were there any business licenses? I keep wondering what Paul meant when he said the brothers had some business ventures."

"Those records aren't at the police station, but I can call a friend at the courthouse tomorrow and ask. I doubt it though, DeDe. Did Paul tell you anything else?"

"They're boyhood pals of Paul's. They went to school together."

"I don't care if they're bosom buddies, I want you to be careful when they're around."

"I will be," Deloris promised, "especially if they've been drinking. Around here they mostly just drink coffee and eat ice cream."

"Good," Austin said. "Now, do you want a ride home?"

"Love one, just let me finish straightening up."

"Are you wearing the apron home?" Austin asked. "Making a fashion statement?"

Deloris rolled her eyes at him and went into the storage room to lock the back door when she saw something white on the floor. She picked it up and realized it was Paul's paycheck. It must have dropped out of his jacket pocket, she thought.

"Austin," she said, "we need to run an errand on the way home."

As Austin and Deloris walked over to the building where the dressing rooms were, they met Stella and Trudie headed in the same direction. Deloris introduced Austin and he offered to give them a ride home, but they declined since Stella's father was coming to pick them up.

CHAPTER 10
The Sullivans

W hile Austin went to bring his car around to the back gate, Deloris hurried to the dressing rooms to change out of her uniform before heading over to the business office. Mr. O'Brien wasn't there, but Deloris was able to convince the night manager to look up Paul's address and give it to her. Once she had it, she dashed outside where Austin was waiting and hopped into his car, explaining about the paycheck.

"So, can we stop by there on the way to Thelma's?" Deloris asked. "Maybe we can learn a little more about Paul or George or even Gordon."

"I think you're chasing fireflies, DeDe," Austin said, "but we'll go check it out."

Deloris and Austin drove to a tiny house on the east side of Kansas City. The house was situated on a narrow street that ended in a dead-end. The porch was sagging and the siding needed a coat of paint, but someone had made the effort to plant flowers in a neat row bordering the porch. Austin waited in the car while Deloris walked up and knocked on the door. A girl about twelve answered the knock.

"Yes?" the girl asked.

"My name is Deloris Markham; I work with Paul Sullivan. Does he live here?"

"Yes'm, that's my older brother, but he's not here right now."

"Paul accidentally left his paycheck at work, so I thought I'd drop it off. Can you give it to him?"

"Yes'm, I can."

Deloris handed over the paycheck. Returning to the car, she told Austin that Paul wasn't home and they could leave. Austin drove down the street to turn around, but as they started to drive back up the street, Deloris saw a familiar face walk up to Paul's door and start knocking. She told Austin to stop and park across the street a little way down from the house.

"Are we doing surveillance now, DeDe?" Austin asked with a grin.

"Hush!" Deloris replied. "I know him, that's Terry Phillips. What is he doing here?"

"Who is Terry?" Austin asked. Deloris explained about Wanda's son, whom she had met at Thelma's door. While they watched, Paul's sister answered the door.

Terry looked agitated when she shook her head, telling him Paul wasn't home. He hit the door jamb above the girl's head and she flinched. He said a few words to her before turning and walking away. Deloris and Austin watched as Terry got into a banged-up brown sedan parked on the side street. The sedan started and took off in a hurry, not even slowing down at the stop sign at the end of the street.

"I wonder what that was about," Deloris broke the silence. "I didn't even know they knew each other."

Austin shook his head as he put the key in the ignition. Before he had even started the car, a dark blue car turned onto the street and pulled into Paul's driveway. Paul got out, as did George and Gordon. Laughing and joking, they walked up to the front door and went inside. A few minutes later they all came running out, jumped in the car and took off.

"That's George and Gordon," Deloris said turning to Austin. "And it doesn't look good. I think we should follow them."

"They're not doing anything illegal," Austin protested, but he started the car and put it in gear. Deloris smiled but didn't say anything. She could see that Austin was just as suspicious as she was.

Keeping a distance, Austin followed the dark blue car until it crossed the state line, headed into Kansas City, Kansas. He pulled off the road and Deloris asked him what was wrong.

"They went into Kansas. I don't have any jurisdiction there."

"Okay, but you can still follow them, can't you? You weren't going to arrest anyone, were you?"

"True, I guess it wouldn't hurt," he replied.

Austin put the car in gear again and continued onward. They could just catch a glimpse of the blue car as it went around a corner at Fifth Street. Austin sped up just in time to see the car turn into a driveway between two buildings. He drove past the building as slowly as he could and they saw the dark blue car parked behind the banged up brown car that Terry had taken off in.

"I wonder what they're up to," Deloris mused.

"Probably nothing," Austin replied, but he kept driving down the street until he found a place to turn around. He parked the car down the hill a little way and they sat there, watching the driveway.

After checking her watch three times and waiting a whole five minutes, Deloris was bored with nothing happening.

"Are you hungry?" she asked.

"Patience, young gumshoe," Austin replied.

Deloris tried to check her makeup, but the streetlights didn't give out enough light for her to see if she needed to powder her nose.

"Okay, if we're just going to sit here, tell me how work went today," she asked.

"Today I was assigned to shadow Big Jim Anderson. He's been a detective for about five years. Hopefully, if all goes well, he'll recommend me for detective one day."

"Wait. What? Are you training with a detective now?"

"Oh yes, I forgot to tell you last night. I've been offered the opportunity to start training as a junior detective now that I finished my probationary one-year period."

"Congratulations! That's great news. Do you like working with him?"

"Absolutely, although I don't know him that well yet. He's quiet, but when he says something, it's worth saying."

"Do you think he will recommend you?"

"Well, I certainly hope so, but he doesn't know me yet, either."

"Is he married?"

"He's dating a teacher at the Kansas City Junior College."

"What about you? Are you seeing anyone?"

"I'm not going to tell you about my love life, Miss Nosey," Austin replied. "But what about you? Are you dating anyone other than Paul, George, and Gordon?"

Deloris squealed and hit him with her purse, "No! I am NOT dating any of them."

"So, how's Poppy's Paradise Park anyway?"

"You've met Stella and Trudie, they're great fun. And I like the job, but I think I need to look for something else."

"Are you quitting?"

"No, I just want a second part-time job. After paying for my room at Thelma's and for the streetcar to get to work, I don't have that much left over from my paycheck. If I get a second job, I'll have spending cash for dresses and shoes, and maybe even some nights out on the town."

"You might also consider a savings account," Austin advised.

"Where's the fun in that?" Deloris replied.

Austin shook his head, and then said, "Look!" pointing up the hill where the trio of George, Gordon and Paul pulled out and took off. A short time later they saw Terry's car leave as well.

"Why aren't you following them?" Deloris asked.

"Because they're not doing anything illegal, and I couldn't arrest them if they were, mostly because it's after midnight and we are still in Kansas. Plus, I have to get up for work tomorrow morning."

"But they could be up to something!"

"Maybe, but all I've seen are a group of guys driving from one location to another."

"Maybe this place has a still and they're making hooch."

"The sign out front says it's a dairy."

"Do they look like milkmen to you?" Deloris demanded.

"Can't say that they do," Austin conceded. "But maybe they're making ice cream. Paul does work at a soda fountain. That could be the business venture."

"At midnight? Wearing suits?" Deloris asked. Austin

tried to find an answer, but couldn't think of anything. "Look," she continued, "can you at least find out what this place is? You know, check to see if it's not an actual dairy."

"I'll look it up tomorrow at work," Austin promised, jotting down the address. "Now, let me drop you off at Thelma's."

"Thanks for tailing those guys," Deloris said. "You're a peach."

"More like a sucker," Austin said, but he was smiling as he said it.

CHAPTER 11

The Switchboard

Monday afternoon, Deloris went downtown to the Kansas City Police Headquarters at 4th and Main, a two-story brick building across the street from the larger, much more imposing City Hall. Deloris went in the front door and up to the large wooden front desk. The placard on the desk identified the man seated behind it as Sergeant Ted Cox, and Deloris asked him if she could see Officer Austin Martin. He told her to wait and he went through a set of doors. A minute later, Sergeant Cox and Austin walked out. The sergeant went back to his seat while Austin headed to Deloris. Before he could say anything, another officer entered with a man in handcuffs and guided him up to the desk. The handcuffed person was yelling, "Let me go! I didn't do nothing wrong. I am innocent!"

Austin turned to Deloris and said, "Let's go back to my desk where it is a little quieter.

"Okay. Whatcha need, kiddo?" he asked.

"First, don't call me kiddo," she replied.

"Do you want my help or not?" Austin said with a wink.

"Yes, I do."

"Okay. What can I do for you, Miss Markham?" he said, putting on his most professional look. "I can call you Miss Markham, can't I?"

Deloris stuck her tongue out at Austin, which caused the sergeant at the desk to snicker. "I want to know if you can help me get a job on the switchboard here."

"Oh, well, I don't know. What are your qualifications?"

"I was an assistant for the telephone operator back in Jameson."

"Covering for my mother once in a while when she ran errands doesn't really count as experience, DeDe," Austin disputed. "You only had a call or two at a time and you only helped so that you could hear the latest gossip."

Deloris glared at him.

"Okay, okay," Austin said. "I really don't know anyone at the switchboard or if they have any openings, but let me ask a few people. Come on back, you can sit in the conference room."

Austin showed her into the room and then left. Deloris sat there looking at the gray walls with framed pictures of President Herbert Hoover and the governor of Missouri—what was his name, Deloris thought to herself—Henry something. Oh yes, Henry Caulfield. Between their pictures was a picture of the American flag. Then she studied the wooden table that had circles on it from people putting down their wet glasses. On one side of the table, it looked like someone laid a cigarette down and allowed it to burn a small circle in the wood. The chairs were a sturdy wood that could withstand the abuse, but the wooden floor had skid marks from the chairs, along with more cigarette burns.

Thank goodness, Austin returned at this point, because

Deloris was starting to get stir crazy and had studied enough of the room to draw a picture. He came back smiling, so he must have learned something, Deloris thought hopefully.

"Good news!" he said as he entered the room with a flourish. "There is an opening at the switchboard. If you go up to the switchboard office on the second floor, ask to speak to Mrs. Mary Virginia Miles. She is expecting you."

"Oh, right now?" Deloris said, surprised.

"Yes," he replied triumphantly.

"I need to comb my hair and check my makeup," she said worriedly.

"You look fine."

"Of course you'd say that."

Austin gave an exaggerated sigh. "Fine. Go back down the hall toward the front desk. Take the hallway on the right, and you'll see the ladies' restroom."

"Thanks, Austin," Deloris said, hurrying down the hallway.

As Deloris checked her makeup in the mirror over the sink, she heard voices and realized that the vent above one of the toilets opened directly into a neighboring room. Bet the architect was a man, she thought, rolling her eyes. She finished up, left the restroom, and headed back down the hall toward the staircase.

"Thank you, Austin," she said as she passed him.

"Just go!" he urged.

Upstairs, Deloris found the door marked switchboard and opened it. Inside the switchboard office, she stopped a moment to look around. The office had light green walls with a gray and white mosaic tile on the floor giving it sort of a drab appearance. With the outside windows on the north side of the building open, the transom over the door to the hallway open, two ceiling fans slowly turning in unison, and a desk fan at every other station, the room was reasonably cool on a hot June day.

She saw five women sitting at the long switchboard, with one vacant seat right in the middle of them. The massive board had wires hanging down from where they were plugged into panels full of holes. The panels only went up an arm's length allowing the women to plug most of them in without standing up. At the base, the unused wires waited to be pulled up, plugged in, and put to use. When the operator finished with the wires, they retracted back into the board. The levers directly in front of the girls completed the connection. On either side of the levers was a pen or pencil and a notepad for the operator to take notes. Each girl had a headset with earphones and a mouthpiece hanging around their neck for them to speak into.

At the end of the switchboard was another door with the word "Manager" written across the glass insert. As Deloris walked behind the women who were seated at their stations, each one turned to watch her go by without missing a beat answering calls. At the door, she knocked and a voice inside the office said, "Yes, come in."

Doing as she was instructed, Deloris opened the door to find a woman of about fifty sitting behind a big wooden desk that took up most of the space in the small office. She stood as Deloris entered the small room. She was tall for a woman, maybe five-foot-eight or -nine with salt and pepper hair that she wore short and straight.

"I'm looking for Mrs. Mary Virginia Miles."

"You've found her." With a pleasant smile, Mary Virginia offered Deloris a seat across from her and sat back down. "How can I help you?"

"Hello, ma'am. My name is Deloris Markham and I

would like to work here at the switchboard. Officer Austin Martin told me to come find you."

"Yes. Do you have any experience working a switchboard?" Mary Virginia asked.

"One of the ladies in the small town where I grew up operated the telephone switchboard out of her house. She was my friend's mother, and when she had a doctor's appointment or needed to run an errand, she would ask me to cover for her sometimes."

"I see. Well, you probably noticed that our operation is much bigger than what you are accustomed to. Speak up and let me hear your voice. I want you to say, '*Kansas City Police Department, what is your emergency, please?*'"

"Kansas City Police Department, what is your emergency, please?"

"Good, good. You have a clear, strong voice with only a slight accent which is easily understood. Where was this small town of yours? Northwest Missouri, right?" Mary Virginia gambled.

"Right, but how did you know?"

"One of my hobbies is listening to people's accents and trying to figure out where they were raised," Mary Virginia said, beaming at her success in nailing another person's accent. "Okay, you're hired. I need you to start this weekend. Can you do that?"

"Oh yes, thank you," Deloris said excitedly as she stood up to leave.

"Alright, the payroll office is directly across the hall from us. I'll call them right now to let them know you're hired. You need to go there and fill out some paperwork. Your hours will be seven o'clock in the morning until two every Saturday and Sunday afternoon. When you work weekends, you get a nickel more per hour."

"Oh," Deloris said before she could stop.

"What's the matter?"

"I was hoping that this job would be full-time or at least during the week. I have another part-time job at Poppy's Paradise Park on the weekend evenings. But I'll take the job, I still want it," Deloris hurriedly assured her.

"I see. None of the girls work full-time. The police department budget hasn't received enough funding for that. We're part of the city budget, and as you know, the economic situation is worse than last year."

"I understand."

"Once I get another girl hired, your hours may change. One of the girls who works for me is quitting next week; she's getting married and moving to Baldwin City. Her shift is Monday through Friday from eight o'clock in the morning until noon. If I can hire someone else to cover the weekend shift, I can move you to that shift. But I have more girls here during the week, so I need to cover the weekend shift first."

"Monday through Friday, eight to noon would be perfect hours for me," Deloris said, and crossed her fingers behind her back, hoping someone else would get hired quickly.

"I like a young woman who is energetic and willing to work two jobs to make ends meet," Mary Virginia said, standing up.

"Thank you," Deloris replied as she turned to leave.

"Oh, one last thing—do you think that you could come in this Friday morning to cover a shift?"

"I should be able to do that," Deloris affirmed.

"Very good. Let me introduce you to some of the girls," Mary Virginia said.

When Mary Virginia walked over to the switchboard, one-by-one each girl turned their swivel stools around to look at who walked in. Mary Virginia introduced Deloris to the girls and told them that she would be working the weekend shift until she could hire someone else to cover that shift. One-by-one they stood up and walked over to Deloris to introduce themselves.

"Hello, I'm Joyce," one said reaching out her hand to shake Deloris's. Joyce had red-hair and freckles like Thelma, so Deloris liked her immediately. "I probably won't see you very much if you are working weekends."

"Oh," Deloris replied disappointedly. "Hello."

"I'm Pam and I'm from the small town of Centerview, Missouri. I don't know why I said that," Pam started laughing.

"That's okay. I'm from a small town, too," Deloris offered. "We can bond over small town jokes." They both laughed.

Pam added, "I won't see you very much either, since I work weekdays."

"I'm Loreda, but they call me Lori." Lori had a warm, welcoming smile. "You are taking my old shift. I just trans-ferred to weekdays last week."

"I'm Beverly, but I prefer that you call me Boo." Boo had a warm, friendly smile but appeared to be a little shy as she quickly turned to go back to her station.

Deloris apologized that she might not remember all of their names right off when Joyce spoke up,

"That's okay sweetie. I've worked here for three years and I still can't remember everyone's name." Then she looked at Pam sitting next to her. "Who are you?"

Pam gave her a soft punch on the shoulder and said, "Oh Joyce, that isn't true and you know it."

Joyce laughed. "I was just trying to make her feel comfortable, Pam. You didn't have to slug me."

As Joyce rubbed her shoulder, Pam retorted, "I didn't hit you that hard."

With various smiles, laughs, and giggles from everyone, including Mary Virginia, the girls all returned to their stations and resumed their duties. As if on cue, the phones started buzzing.

Mary Virginia said, "Well, you'd better get over to the payroll office and get signed up. I'll see you on Friday."

After completing the paperwork in the payroll office, Deloris headed back downstairs, happy she had another job. The hours weren't great, but at least she had a chance that they would change if they hired another girl. Then it'd be almost perfect.

Downstairs, before leaving the police station, Deloris stopped by Austin's office to tell him the good news. He offered his congratulations, and then said, "There's one other thing. I looked up the address where Paul, George, Gordon, and Terry were last night. It really is a dairy; they deliver all around here. Maybe that actually is a legitimate business venture."

"Do you really believe that?"

"I'm a detective-in-training, DeDe. I have to use the facts."

"I understand," Deloris said, noting that he hadn't actually answered her question.

CHAPTER 12

Good News Then Bad

Deloris waited until Thelma came home from work at Leed's Lunch Counter, and then she pulled everyone into the living room to tell them the good news about her new job. She started twirling Annie around the dining room while Wanda and Thelma laughed at their dancing. Everyone was excited for her except Leota, who complained about the ruckus and went upstairs. The din from everyone talking at once reached a high pitch, but when the phone rang in the hallway, they quieted down so that Annie, who answered the phone, could hear. She told Thelma it was for her and returned to the table.

Thelma seldom received phone calls except from family and when they called it was usually bad news, so she approached the phone cautiously. Deloris stayed by the kitchen door, eavesdropping, in case something had happened to one of their relatives.

"Hello? Oh, hello, Marguerite. How are you?"

Marguerite told Thelma her bad news about the robbery and how she and Tommy had been tied up.

"What? Are you okay? Is Tommy okay?" Thelma asked.

When she heard the concern in her sister's voice, Deloris moved nearer to Thelma so she could listen more intently to the one-sided conversation. Thelma motioned for her to come closer and turned the phone's earpiece sideways in order for Deloris to listen to Marguerite's story.

Marguerite replied, "I'm okay, just shaken up and Tommy is feeling better from his chicken pox but he isn't out of the woods yet. It is his fifth day with them, so he can still be contagious."

"Well, I'm glad that you both are okay."

Marguerite continued, "The police just left and I need to go the hospital for the doctor to do a quick check-up. He wants me to come back tomorrow for a more thorough exam."

"How is Harry?" Thelma persisted.

"Harry is upset and wants to hunt down the intruders and take them out of this world for hurting us. But I managed to convince him to let the police investigate."

"Oh dear. I understand how he feels. What can I do to help you?"

"It would be helpful if you or one of your girls could come over and watch Tommy while we go to the hospital. We haven't made it public yet, but I'm pregnant. That's why the doctor wants a more thorough exam tomorrow. Then Harry and I need to go to the police station to make a more formal statement and give a preliminary list of what was stolen, and I need to sit with a sketch artist and give a description."

"Oh Marguerite. I don't know what to say. I am so happy for you and Harry, but I'm also concerned. I need to finish making dinner for my boarders but I am certain that

Deloris or one of the other girls can help you out. What time do you need someone to be there?"

Marguerite answered, "We will leave as soon as someone can get here to watch Tommy."

Deloris nodded and headed upstairs to grab her purse and hat.

"Okay, Deloris will be there soon. Sit tight. Goodbye."

When Thelma got off the phone, she shared the story with everyone else. Annie started interrupting Thelma every few words by asking questions.

Thelma couldn't answer them all, but she told Annie, "Deloris is going to leave as soon as possible to babysit Tommy so that Marguerite and Harry can go to the hospital and police station. When she returns, she can fill us all in."

Deloris glided quickly down the stairs and ran into the kitchen to grab a roll. Thelma told her that she would put a plate of food in the icebox for her to eat later. She also handed her a few coins for a taxi, which Deloris gladly accepted, giving her sister a quick hug. Annie called for the taxi and told them it was an emergency.

When the taxi arrived, Deloris flew out of the front door. She jumped into the backseat of the awaiting taxi and said, "Okay, I'm ready." But the driver didn't take off. He looked a little concerned at her urgency and patiently waited for the address.

"Oh, the address."

Deloris jumped out of the taxi and ran back toward the house, since even though she had been to Marguerite's a few times, she didn't know the address. Thelma, realizing that she hadn't given it to her, was running out of the house yelling after her. Thelma handed her the address and Deloris hurried back to the taxi.

Giving the taxi driver the address, she asked him to step

on it. He took off so fast that it threw Deloris across the seat, slamming her back into the door on the other side of the car. Her back started to hurt from where she'd injured it in the car crash with Walter and she was afraid that she would reinjure it. She managed to grab ahold of the strap in the door in the backseat and lean forward.

"I appreciate your enthusiasm, but could you slow down just a little?"

"Yes, ma'am."

As the taxi made its way to Marguerite's house, Deloris thought about Marguerite and Thelma. From the outside, the two women led very different lives, but they had been friends since they were children in a little one-room schoolhouse near Jameson, Missouri. Thelma didn't go beyond eighth grade because her momma needed her to help with her younger siblings and orphaned cousins. Marguerite continued on to high school and graduated, then moved to Kansas City to live with an elderly aunt. She met Harry when accompanying her aunt to the bank where Harry worked. Thelma and Marguerite remained close friends through the years, and when Thelma also moved to Kansas City, Marguerite helped her get settled and secure a job at the egg factory. Deloris didn't know Marguerite that well growing up since Marguerite was a senior when Deloris was in kindergarten, but she'd met her sister's best friend several times afterward when she accompanied Thelma and her daughters to Marguerite's house while Harry was at work.

As they pulled up outside of Marguerite's home, Deloris saw that every light in the house was on and a police car was still in the driveway. She paid the taxi driver, ran up the front walkway, and knocked on the door. Harry flung it open and the police officer inside quickly turned to face the door. Deloris, who had never met Harry, quickly explained to him that she was Thelma's sister there to babysit his son.

"Thank God," he said as Marguerite slowly came down the stairs. She had a black eye starting to form and her cheek was still red where the robber had slapped her. Her wrists had marks on them from being tied up and something seemed to be wrong with her knee as she hobbled down the stairs.

"Oh Deloris, thank you for coming so quickly," Marguerite said, "I know that I look a fright." She put one hand up to her hair as if to check for any strands that were out of place.

Before Deloris could say anything, Harry handed Marguerite her coat and whisked her out the door. After a second, Deloris ran to the door and called out, "Where is Tommy?"

Marguerite turned and started to walk back, but Harry stopped her so she pointed, "He's upstairs, first bedroom on the left."

"Okay," Deloris answered, waving them onward to their mission.

CHAPTER 13
From the Mouths of Babes

D eloris closed the door and went upstairs to look in
on Tommy. He was sitting up in his bed, intently
reading the comic strip section of the newspaper.
Tommy looked up at the door and was slightly startled to
see Deloris standing there. As she entered the room, he put
the newspaper down and watched her walk to the side of
his bed.

"I'm sorry if I scared you. I'm Deloris, Thelma's sister.
Do you remember me?"

"Oh, that's all right. I remember you. I wasn't scared,
just didn't know anyone was standing there," Tommy said
with bravado.

"What are you reading?" Deloris asked. She thought
that it would be a good icebreaker to get to know him better,
since she had only met him once when he and his mother
came to visit Thelma.

"Detective Dick Percy," was Tommy's reply.

"So, you like Detective Percy?" Deloris continued, as
she pulled up a chair to his bedside.

"Oh, yes," he answered. "He is the smartest detective in the world. I want to grow up to be just like him someday."

"I've never read Detective Dick Percy. Tell me about him."

"He's only the best detective ever. He catches all of the criminals and says, *'Criminals always get caught'* as he hauls them off to jail," Tommy offered.

"Well, that is true."

"No, that is Detective Percy's motto. *'Criminals always get caught.'"*

"Oh, I see."

Tommy continued eagerly, "Yeah, he joined the police force after his girlfriend's father was murdered by robbers and they kidnapped his girlfriend."

"My goodness!" Deloris exclaimed. "That sounds horrible."

With his eyes lit up at the chance to talk about his favorite detective, Tommy quickly replied, "Yeah."

Deloris could see that he was excited to share his favorite comic strip with an adult who was actually listening to him.

He went on, "It sounds exactly like what happened to Mommy and me. Well except no one was kidnapped or murdered."

"That is true, thankfully," Deloris confirmed. "Let's hope the police detectives find the guys who did this to you and your momma and put them away for a long time."

"I wanted to tell the officers about the bad guys, but no one wanted to talk to me," Tommy muttered, looking down dejectedly.

"Really? Well, I'm listening. You can tell me," Deloris offered. Just in case he said something that might be interesting, she grabbed a pencil and a piece of paper from her purse and leaned in a little.

"Okay, well, the one guy had a missing tooth right in the front, here," Tommy said, pointing at one of the teeth in his mouth. Deloris recalled that it was called a canine tooth because it was longer than the rest.

"I bit him on the arm and drew blood," Tommy said proudly. "I also gave him a punch in the gut and he doubled over for a moment, but then came back up and sucker-punched me in the stomach." Tommy was very proud of the fight he put up to save his mother. "Also, they didn't get my money that was in my piggy bank," Tommy said victoriously, satisfied that he had outsmarted the crooks.

"Very good, Tommy," Deloris offered encouragingly.

Pleased with himself, Tommy continued, "The other guy was wearing a ring on his pinky finger."

"That is very interesting." Tommy had Deloris's full attention. "What did it look like?"

"It was black with a face in the middle of it and the ring part was gold."

"Tommy, you are a good detective already and very observant. If it's okay with you, I will tell this information to one of my friends who is a police detective just like Detective Percy."

"Really? Gosh, do you think that I can meet him?"

"I am certain that he and his partner will be more than happy to come and see you," Deloris said with a big smile. "Now, you had better turn your light out and get some sleep so that you will feel better in the morning."

"Oh, I feel just fine now," Tommy said, looking up at Deloris with his chicken pox still visible among the freckles across his face. Deloris had heard Marguerite tell Thelma this was the fifth day for his chicken pox so he should be over them soon, but Deloris made sure not to get too close to him in case he was still contagious. She had the chicken pox when she was a child, though, so she thought she should be immune from catching them again. Still, she erred on the side of caution.

When she started to turn out the light, Tommy asked if she could leave it on, a most understandable request after the scary day he had.

Deloris went downstairs and sat on the couch to wait for Marguerite and Harry to return. She picked up a *Ladies' Home Journal* magazine from the coffee table and flipped through the pages, not really reading or looking at what was in front of her. She turned on the radio, but hearing nothing but static, she turned it off and returned to the magazine.

What was that? She heard a noise. Was it at the back door? She stood up and looked around for a weapon. Grabbing a fireplace poker, she cautiously moved toward the back of the house turning off lights as she went. When she got to the back door, she looked out the window at the side and gazed into the Adcocks' backyard. She didn't see anyone or anything, so she lowered the poker and carefully opened the door. In a rush, a black cat came dashing into the kitchen, frightening Deloris half to death. This must be the family cat that Harry originally thought was in the basement. Closing the door, Deloris made certain that it was locked and bolted. The cat started rubbing up against her leg purring softly.

"*Achoo*—look kitty—*achoo*—I like you—*achoo*, but I can't help you," she said as the sneezing commenced. "You need—*achoo*—to stay over there." Pointing to the pile of rags that was obviously its bed, Deloris realized that it was futile trying to get the cat away. She opened the icebox and found a bottle of milk. Pouring some of it into bowl, she placed it near the cat's bed. Quickly walking away, she retrieved the poker and closed the kitchen door behind her.

Thankfully, she heard Harry and Marguerite entering the front door as she entered the living room. Marguerite saw her with the poker and looked concerned.

Deloris quickly replaced the fireplace poker and put the magazine back on the coffee table. "Oh, nothing of concern happened," she reassured Marguerite. "I heard a noise at the back door, so I grabbed the poker, but it was just a black cat. I gave it some milk and left it in the kitchen. I'm allergic to cats and had to shut the door to keep it in there."

Harry quickly remarked, "That damn cat is always underfoot. We need to get rid of him."

With a sigh, Marguerite answered in a calming tone, "Now Harry, you always say that, but you know that Tommy loves the cat. Getting rid of it would break his heart."

"I know, but I can dream, can't I?" Harry said with a smile. The cat conversation was a comfortable one that obviously had taken place many times before and helped to ease the tension from the excitement of the day.

Marguerite turned to Deloris and offered her some coins for babysitting. Deloris politely declined her offer but asked if she could get a ride home.

"Most definitely, my dear. That is the least we can do. Harry, will you take Deloris home?"

"Sure thing," he said as he got his keys and jumped to open the front door for Deloris. On the ride home, Deloris asked Harry if he had any idea who would have robbed and beaten up his wife and son.

"I don't have any idea, but as the vice president of a bank you always run the risk of someone trying to rob you. I try to keep my home life very private and seldom bring my wife to any office functions. Only one or two people even have my home address," Harry said thoughtfully.

"Who are they?"

"Oh, just my secretary, and the president, of course."

"What did they take?" Deloris continued.

"Mostly silver," Harry replied. "Oh, and Marguerite's wedding ring and some other jewelry, but she is the most upset about the wedding ring."

"I don't blame her. Have you seen any strange cars in your neighborhood or following you?"

"No, the police asked me the same questions. I really haven't paid much attention. There could have been and I just didn't notice them," Harry replied.

"Well, if I were you, I'd pay a little closer attention from now on. Just in case they come back," Deloris offered. "Oh, one more thing, was your wife able to describe the robbers?"

"She said that it all happened so fast, but she did tell the police that she remembered one guy was wearing a uniform like the electric power people wear, and the other guy was wearing gray coveralls like a mechanic would wear. She didn't get a good look at their faces. She did manage to scratch the one guy on his arm and maybe on the neck or face."

"She didn't notice anything else about them?"

"Not that I heard her say. Why do you want to know?"

"Oh, I fancy myself a sort of detective and I am always interested in the details."

"Well, I'm sure the police can handle it," Harry said dismissively as he pulled up in front of Thelma's house. "Here we are."

"Oh yes, thank you for the lift, Mr. Adcock," Deloris said as she exited the vehicle.

Once inside, Deloris thought that from what Marguerite told the police and what Tommy said, they should have several clues to catch the culprits. "Out of the mouths of babes," she said to no one in particular.

CHAPTER 14

Detectives

The next morning after breakfast, Deloris took a streetcar to the police station to tell Austin what she had learned from Tommy and to see if they had any leads. As luck would have it, Austin was sitting at the front desk.

"Austin, what are you doing here?"

"I'm the rookie so I get to cover for Sergeant Cox because has the day off."

"I see," Deloris said with a smile. "Well, this is better anyway because I need to tell you something."

"Okay," he said. At that moment the phone rang and interrupted. Austin held up a finger as if to say wait and answered the phone. "Yes, yes, okay. Got it." He hung up the phone, but not before writing something down. "Hold on, DeDe. I need to handle this first."

"Okay."

He flipped a switch and spoke into a microphone, "Calling all cars. Calling all cars. Robbery at 815 Broadway." Then he stood up and went to the door to the squad room and yelled, "Robbery at 815 Broadway!"

From the interior, someone yelled back, "On my way!"

He returned to the desk and said, "Now, what were you saying?" without looking up from writing on the same pad of paper.

She walked closer to the desk which was much higher than the average desk, giving Austin the advantage of looking down at whomever was in front of him. There was a partial wall about waist high that ran from the side of the desk to the wall with a swinging door that anyone entering the main room had to walk through. Deloris put her hand on the desk to get his attention and he looked up from writing.

"Sorry, DeDe. It is just that working this desk is crazy. I don't know how Ted keeps everything straight. What were you saying?"

"What was that all about?"

"Another robbery. It is the second one today."

"Do you need to go investigate?"

"No, I need to stay at the front desk today. Someone else will handle it."

"But this won't help you move on to detective, will it?"

"No, but it's only for a day. What did you want?"

"Oh, I was going to tell you about some new evidence from the robbery at the Adcock home. I babysat last night while Mr. and Mrs. Adcock came here to give their statements and I talked to them about what happened."

"Oh, I'm not working that case. Tim, I mean, Detective O'Malley is."

"So do I need to talk with him?" Deloris asked.

"Yes, let me call him up here." Austin opened the door behind him and called for Detective O'Malley to come to the front desk.

Timothy O'Malley was a man of about sixty, short and

rotund with a round face and a balding head. When he saw Deloris, his eyes lit up like a child looking at candy. Giving her the glad eye, he said,"Well, hello there dollface, did you want to see me?"

Ignoring his leer, Deloris said, "Yes, I have some information on the Adcock Family robbery."

"Oh, you do, do you?" he said a little suspiciously. "Were you involved?" he said with a wink to Austin, who quickly wiped the smirk off his face when he saw Deloris glaring at him.

"No, of course not," Deloris replied, annoyed that he wasn't taking her seriously. "I talked with the family and learned some additional details that I don't believe you have."

"We already have their statements," Detective O'Malley said dismissively.

"Yes, I know, but I don't believe you talked with the son," Deloris insisted.

"He's just a kid. What could he know?"

"You'd be surprised at what he knows," Deloris said.

O'Malley groaned and said, "You fancy yourself an Agatha Christie or something?" He turned to Austin again and said, "My wife reads that baloney and thinks she's a sleuth, always offering me advice." He ended the statement with a guffaw.

Deloris could see that he wasn't going to take her seriously, so she stepped back and said, "Never mind. I'm sure you have all the information you need to solve the case. Sorry to bother you."

Detective O'Malley let out a satisfied harrumph and turned to Austin saying, "Ain't it just like a dame to waste a man's time. They got nothing better to do." Before Austin could respond, he turned and walked back to his desk.

Deloris was furious at this encounter and decided then and there that any proper investigating on this case would need to be done by her. She couldn't see letting Marguerite down by letting this clown work her case—he'd never solve the mystery. Those thugs were still out there somewhere, and Deloris decided this was her next goal: she'd find the robbers and turn them over to the police.

Before she stormed out of the police station she turned and gave Austin one last angry look. He shrugged and shook his head with a look that said, "There's nothing I can do."

When Austin got off work, he stopped by Thelma's to apologize to Deloris for Detective O'Malley's behavior.

He pleaded his case, "Look, DeDe, I'm a rookie. I can't talk back to the senior detectives like Tim O'Malley. He is close to retiring, wields a lot of power, and is pretty set in his ways. I could lose my job if I talked back to him and I definitely wouldn't make full detective. In fact, I'd be busted back down to walking the streets."

"I understand," Deloris said. "He just made me so furious, treating me like a silly little school girl or a second-class citizen."

"I know. I don't like it, but I just need to stay out of trouble until he retires. He could recommend that I not be promoted to full detective and that would sink my chances to ever make detective. Remember, I'm still only a junior detective," Austin said, looking apologetic.

"Well, will you at least listen to what I have to say?"

"I'm not sure I can do anything with it, but of course I'll listen," Austin replied.

"Okay, well first, Tommy is eight years old and fancies himself an amateur detective. He is a big fan of Detective Dick Percy"

Austin groaned a little before saying, "Go on."

"I told him that you and your partner would be willing to talk with him someday."

"Okay," Austin said, looking impatient.

"Okay, well, he said that one of the guys was missing a tooth and he pointed to this one," Deloris said, pointing at her tooth like Tommy did.

At this, Austin pulled a note pad and pencil out of his jacket pocket. He wrote this down and said, "Okay, that might actually be helpful information... Is there more?"

"Yes," Deloris said eagerly. "The other guy had a gold ring on his pinky finger with a dark stone like a black onyx, I think with a cameo etched into it."

"Okay, got it."

"Oh, and he said that he bit the guy with the missing tooth on the arm and drew blood."

"These are actually good leads, DeDe," Austin said, surprised.

"I know," Deloris said, proud of finally getting someone to listen to her, just like Tommy.

"What I can do is share this information with Captain Elden Denton and let him use it to help find the culprits. Rumor has it that he is in to be the next chief when our current chief retires."

Satisfied that something was going to be done, Deloris said, "That sounds like a good idea."

"All right," Austin said as he stood up to leave.

"Oh, don't forget that I promised Tommy that you or your partner would talk with him about being a detective."

"I'll see what I can do on that, too." At that, Austin walked out the door.

CHAPTER 15

On the Job

F riday morning, Deloris arrived for her first shift at the switchboard ten minutes early. She walked in and was greeted by Mary Virginia, who was standing there talking with one of the girls.

Mary Virginia pointed at the middle vacant seat so Deloris took her place and put on the headset. Mary Virginia gave her some brief instructions on the switchboard and went back to her office. Almost immediately, Deloris's station buzzed, and she plugged in the wire and flipped the switch to connect.

"Kansas City Police Department, what is your emergency, please?"

"Hey, it's me, Austin. I was just checking to see how it's going."

"Oh, hey. You are my first call, but you know I can't have any personal calls while I'm at work," Deloris said in a lower voice so that hopefully no one noticed that it was personal.

"I know. I won't take too long. I just wanted to tell you that I gave the information to Captain Denton and he was most interested in the onyx cameo ring. It seems that it matches the description of a ring that was stolen in a house robbery two weeks ago."

"Really?"

"Yeah. Oh, gotta go. Tim, I mean Detective O'Malley, just walked up."

"Okay. Bye."

Joyce, who was sitting next to her, turned to say in a low voice, "Careful about personal calls. There is a phone in the back that you can use when you're on your break, but it gets pretty busy because we take breaks in shifts and two girls go at a time."

"I'll keep that in mind," Deloris said. Then she added, "That was a police detective telling me about a case." Austin was already a full-fledged detective to her anyway, she thought with a smile.

"Oh, well, he can come up here in person and say it is for police business and you can talk with him at the back of the room or outside. That is allowed."

"That's good to know," Deloris replied.

"No problem, sweetie." Then Joyce took a call and started writing down the details.

At that moment Deloris's board started buzzing again. She plugged the wire in, flipped the switch and said,

"Kansas City Police Department, what is your emergency, please?"

The voice on the other end of the call started crying. "My husband was just shot!"

"Calm down, ma'am, and give me details. Is he still breathing?"

"Yes, but barely." The voice became muffled, but Deloris heard the woman say, "Hang in there, baby. I'm getting help."

"Did you call the hospital for an ambulance?"

"What? Oh yes, and they told me to call the police. Hurry, please."

"Where are you?"

"111 St. John."

"Okay, ma'am. I'll send someone there immediately."

She disconnected the call and turned to Boo. "How do I send the police to an emergency?"

"Oh, no one showed you that? See this button here?" Boo responded.

In the middle of the board was a place to plug a wire in and push a button, clearly marked *Front Desk*. When Deloris pushed the button, she remembered the face of the friendly desk sergeant.

"Front Desk, Sergeant Cox."

"Sergeant Cox, I have a gunshot victim at 111 St. John. The ambulance has been called."

"We'll get on it right away," he said, and hung up.

Deloris leaned back and took a deep breath.

"Wow, you got a hot one right out of the chute," Boo said, wide-eyed.

"I know," Deloris said. "I hope I did okay."

"Sounded good on my end."

"Thanks."

After the shooting call, the day went by quickly with non-emergency calls such as a peeping tom, a noise complaint, and a fender-bender traffic accident. When noon came, Deloris took off the earphones and mouthpiece and stood up, stretching her back. The swivel chair's metal back rest wasn't that comfortable for someone with a bad back. Before she left, she asked Mary Virginia if she could bring a pillow tomorrow to put behind her back and received permission. She then went downstairs to find Austin but met him on the stairs coming up.

"Oh, I was just coming down to see you," Deloris said.

"I thought that I would see if you wanted to go to lunch," Austin offered.

"Yes, that'd be swell," she answered.

They went to the Woolworth's lunch counter and were surprised to see a fellow from their hometown eating there. Dr. David Kerns sat at a table with another man. When he saw Deloris and Austin, he motioned for them to come to his table.

"I haven't seen you in years!" Deloris exclaimed.

"I haven't been back to Jameson much, what with finishing medical school and then starting a practice," David explained. "Your brother, Roy, wrote me that you were coming to the city and I've been intending to check on you."

He then introduced them to Dr. Jeremiah Browne, his medical practice partner. They all exchanged pleasantries, and David suggested that they should all go to lunch sometime. Deloris and Austin agreed, and then walked over to the counter to order while David and Jeremiah resumed eating their meal.

The long counter at Woolworth's was bustling with people, and while they were waiting for the cashier to take their order Austin looked up at the menu board behind the counter. Deloris looked around at what others were eating. The chicken fried steak with buttered green beans looked good, and so did the meatloaf with whipped potatoes, gravy, and salad. Deloris decided to order the meatloaf while Austin got a ham salad sandwich and a bowl of vegetable soup.

As Deloris and Austin ate, she told him about her first emergency call, and he told her that he and Big Jim had been the ones assigned to investigate. "Apparently it was a mob hit. The victim didn't pay up on his 'protection fee' and they sent him a message."

"What's a 'protection fee?'" she asked.

"Mobsters extort money out of honest store owners by telling them that they need to pay them a protection fee to keep them from shooting up, bombing, or robbing the business, or even killing the owner."

"Oh," Deloris said with a touch of fright. "Did the shooting victim survive?"

"It looks like he will."

"Thank goodness."

Deloris was in a good mood as she headed home to take a nap after lunch. She found working the switchboard at the police department an exciting job. It put her in the know of what was going on in the heart of Kansas City. The only thing she didn't like was the hours, since they meant long days between getting up early for the switchboard and working late into the evening at Poppy's Paradise Park. She was determined to find another switchboard operator for Mary Virginia to hire, so that she could move to the weekday shift.

When she got home, Deloris headed upstairs, hoping to fall into bed and catch a quick shuteye before going to the soda fountain. Annie had her door open, though, and with a finger to her lips, indicated that Deloris needed to come quietly into her bedroom. Though the curtains were closed, Annie's window was open, and there were voices coming from the alley below.

Deloris peeked out the window to see Wanda, Terry,

and a girl standing below them at the garage door. With what was probably a broken nose covered by a bandage and maybe a black eye or two that Deloris couldn't quite make out in the dim light, Terry's appearance really piqued her interest. She carefully closed the curtain and Annie moved closer so that they both could hear the conversation below.

"What happened to your face?" Wanda asked worriedly.

"Never mind that, Ma. I need some money so that Maizie and I can get married and get out of this town."

"Terry, honey, you need to think this through. Where will you go? What will you do? What do you really know about this girl?"

"I know that I love her and I want to marry her. That's all I need to know."

"Don't do anything rash that you might regret later."

"Ma . . ." Terry let out an exhausted breath.

"Let's go, sugar," put in Maizie "This old battleax isn't going to help us. Let's go ask one of your friends to loan us the money. They always got lots of cabbage to throw around like it's easy to come by."

"Maizie, listen, I can't ask them. I already owe Babyface and Brown a lot of moolah. Why do you think they beat me up? I also owe Paul. If I go back to them for money, Babyface will take a pound of it out in flesh, maybe two pounds. Why do you think we need to get out of this town? I need to get the money from Ma." Terry turned and looked at his mother pleadingly.

"Terry, dear," Wanda interrupted. "I can't give you any money tonight. I don't have any on me. Think this through. You don't need to marry her. You can just leave town instead."

"I'll be back tomorrow, Ma, and I need you to have the

money ready."

Peeking out the window again, Deloris saw Terry and Maizie storm off toward the side street where they must have parked to avoid detection by anyone at Thelma's.

From the porch light above Wanda's door, they could see that she was seething with anger and heard her muttering to herself as she walked back to the house. Wanda glanced up at the open window and they quickly ducked behind the curtain again. After witnessing this interaction, Annie told Deloris about Wanda's son, "Terry the Terror," they called him. "He is always coming to beg for money over and over again, but this time he looked like he had been beaten up pretty badly."

"So this happens often?" Deloris asked.

"Yes, I've seen him in the alley a couple of times. Wanda pleads with him to quit hanging around his friends, but he just takes her money and leaves."

"Oh, really."

Deloris wondered if Terry's injuries happened when she saw George, Gordon, and Paul follow him to the dairy the other night. She wanted to stay and talk more with Annie, but she was bone-tired and needed some sleep. She told Annie that she would talk with Wanda and try to find out more information, and headed to her room for a much-needed nap.

After her nap, Deloris found Wanda in the dining room and sat down to talk with her.

"Wanda, are you okay? You look upset," Deloris began, trying to appear nonchalant and not as a witness to the earlier conversation.

"Oh, I just get upset with my son from time to time, but he's a good boy. He's just a poor judge of people's character."

"It's hard. People can fool you if you aren't careful. Tell me about your son."

Wanda's face changed as she thought about Terry. "I lost Terry's father some years ago, so I have had to raise him by myself. It's hard, you know, raising a child by yourself. When he was about ten years old, I got a job at the bank and had to leave him at home alone after school. That's when he started hanging out with Gordon and George Nelson."

Deloris then asked her, "So Terry knows Paul, George, and Gordon from school?"

"Yes, they went to school together. Well, really just Paul and George went to school with my Terry. Gordon was a little younger. Paul used to be Terry's best friend. They played together when they were younger, before George transferred to the school. We used to have Paul over to our house all the time, for Terry's birthdays and for sleepovers. Those were good times. But when George showed up, Paul started running with him and dropped Terry like a hot potato."

At this, Wanda started crying. "Those boys have always been bad news. I wish they'd never moved to our neighborhood and now they beat Terry up again. How could they do that to my Terry?" she asked Deloris, who could only shake her head.

So, Wanda just confirmed that Gordon, George, and Paul did give Terry a thrashing, Deloris thought to herself. Wanda still looked angry at the thought of them and became agitated again.

"Can I get you some tea or coffee?" Deloris offered, hoping to keep her talking.

"Coffee would be nice."

"Did Terry say why they hit him?"

"Not really," Wanda replied between sobs. "They don't need a reason. They even followed my Terry to his work at the dairy and mugged him there."

"I see," Deloris replied, knowing that he did say he owed them money. She pressed Wanda anyway to get more information. "But he didn't say why they did it?"

"Well, they've always bullied my boy. They used to beat him up at school, too. I complained to their grandmother, but the next day they just lay into him more, so I quit complaining. Then one day, Gordon fought with a neighbor kid and the kid's parents had to rush him to the hospital. Gordon took off and the officers couldn't find him. A week later George disappeared, too, and I said good riddance. Then they reappeared about five years later. They both have always been bad seeds, I tell you."

"Did Paul stay in school and resume his friendship with Terry?"

"Yes, he graduated with Terry, but their friendship just wasn't the same. Although, occasionally Paul would come by and invite Terry to hang out, and Terry would be so happy."

"Is Terry going to file charges?"

"No, they'd probably kill him if he went to the police. Why are you asking so many questions?"

"I'm just concerned about you and thought it might help you to talk about it and get some things off your mind."

At that, Deloris quit asking Wanda questions. She didn't want to tell her that she saw Paul, George, and Gordon when they beat Terry up. She would probably want to know why Deloris didn't call the police or try to stop them.

CHAPTER 16
Friends and Suspicions

That Friday night was the start of the summer season at Poppy's Paradise Park. Paul and Deloris were both scheduled to work at the soda fountain until closing time every weekend until the end of July. Mr. O'Brien explained that, June and July were the busiest months with the biggest crowds at the park. After schools started up in August, things would slow back down a bit and only one person would be scheduled to work until the park closed for the winter after Labor Day weekend.

True to her first experience with Paul, as soon as Deloris started working on Friday evening, Paul left, leaving her to deal with the crowds and to clean up the mess after the soda fountain closed. Even though Deloris didn't really like the way Paul expected her to cover for him, she did like working at the park. There were live bands on the weekends, and she loved listening to the music and talking with all of her customers.

Right after Paul left, Trudie and Stella stopped by, smelling like popcorn and cotton candy. "We can't stay long, we're on break," Stella explained, "but we decided we needed ice cream tonight. It's just too hot out there."

"What'll you have?" asked Deloris.

Trudie looked at the menu board on the wall above Deloris. "How about a Canary Island Special?"

"And a Double Chocolate Malt for me," Stella chimed in.

As Deloris made their orders, the girls chatted about the weather and the events at the park, including the end-of-summer bash being planned for Labor Day weekend.

"Do you have anything lined up for September?" Stella asked. "I'm going back to be a housemaid for this ritzy couple that lives on Ward Parkway. They went to Europe for the summer and I had the whole house to myself which is why I took the job here. I could work at my family's restaurant but I don't want to do that yet."

"I don't know what I'll do after Labor Day," Deloris said. "I was happy to find this job, and I just got another part-time job at the police switchboard on Saturdays and Sundays. But I'll need to find another job to replace this one at the end of summer. Do you think that I could work at your family's restaurant?"

"Maybe so. I'll ask."

"I hope you can work there or find something else," Trudie said. "Maybe you can go to work at another soda fountain."

"What are you going to do?" Deloris asked Trudie.

"My aunt works at a dressmaker's factory. I've been practicing sewing with her all summer and she says I'm almost good enough to apply there."

When Stella and Trudie left, a group of schoolkids came in. They all wanted ice cream cones, and as soon as they had them, they immediately ran back outside. Deloris had several customers and hardly had time to clean up after each one. Close to closing time, as Deloris was wiping up the spatters of ice cream left on the counter, a young woman with long blonde hair and green eyes came in.

Deloris asked, "Can I help you?"

"I hope so," the woman responded. "Would it be all right if I stayed in here a while to listen to the music? My friends don't like jazz, so they left early, and I didn't want to wander around the park by myself."

"Of course you can stay," Deloris smiled. "If you don't mind, I'll pull up a chair and listen with you until I get another customer. I love this music."

The young woman agreed and introduced herself as Gracie Burnett. They started chatting, and Deloris, still thinking about Stella's question of where she would work in September, asked Gracie what she did.

"I don't have a job, actually," Gracie replied. "I'm from Sedalia and I'm visiting friends in Kansas City while I look for a place to stay. I've been admitted to the Kansas City Junior College. I'm lucky enough to have parents who can pay for me to go to college. I'd still like to get a job, though, so that my parents don't have to cover my rent on top of tuition."

"I know just the place," Deloris said, and told Gracie all about Thelma's boarding house. "If you're interested, I'll check with Thelma in the morning, and then call you to let you know what time to come by."

"That sounds perfect!" Gracie said, and she made plans with Deloris to visit the house the next afternoon after Deloris got home from working at the switchboard.

Deloris got up early on Saturday morning, yawning from the short night of sleep. She hadn't gotten home from Poppy's until late and she wanted to get up early to talk to Thelma before her shift at the switchboard started. Deloris brewed some strong coffee, and as she sipped it, a grin broke across her face. She'd figured out a way to move to the weekday shift at the switchboard.

When Thelma got up, she came into the kitchen to start breakfast and found Deloris there.

"Good morning, Thelma. I found a new potential boarder for you," Deloris said with a lilt of excitement in her voice.

"That's great news. Who is it?"

"I met a girl at the park last night who was in town looking for a place to live while she goes to college. She's from Sedalia and is also looking for a job."

"Oh, really? The Missouri State Fair is held there. I always thought that one day I'd like to go and take the girls," Thelma said wistfully. "Anyway, when do I get to meet her?"

"I can have her here this afternoon. I just need to give her a call to give her the address."

"Okay. Do it."

Deloris ran to the phone and called Gracie to confirm that she could come over to look at the room that afternoon.

"Also," Deloris said to Gracie, "I may have found a job for you. Do you know anything about telephone switchboards? I can get you an interview."

"No, I'm afraid that I don't, and I do need to go home Sunday night."

"That isn't a problem," Deloris reassured her. "If Mary Virginia agrees to an interview tomorrow morning, I can teach you this afternoon, it's easy."

When Deloris went into work that Saturday morning, she found Mary Virginia there. She was planning to call her, but this was better. She preferred talking to her face-to-face.

"Don't you go home?" Deloris said, laughing.

"Oh, good morning, Deloris. Yes, I do. I just came in to get a few things that I left on my desk."

"This is good. I was going to call you today, but now I don't need to."

"You aren't quitting already, are you?"

"Oh, goodness no, but I think that I found a girl to work the weekend shift so that way I can switch to the weekday shift.

"Does she know how to operate a switchboard?"

"Yes, she is a little rusty on it, but I'm going to help her this afternoon to refresh her skills." It was just a little lie, Deloris thought to herself. "Her name is Gracie Burnett."

Mary Virginia agreed to interview Gracie Sunday afternoon, promising that if she was as good as Deloris on the switchboard, she'd be hired.

She'll be exactly as good as me, Deloris thought, because I'm the one who'll teach her.

As Deloris walked up to Thelma's house that afternoon after her shift, she saw Walter hanging around the back door. She started to walk back there to ask him what he was doing, but when he saw her he ducked and took off in a hurry. She shrugged her shoulders and went inside. She found Gracie was already there.

"What was Walter doing here?" she asked Thelma.

"Walter? I didn't see him."

"Well, I just saw him around the back and when he saw me, he took off like a shot."

Thelma groaned. "I'll talk with him again."

Gracie's visit to Thelma's house that afternoon went well. Thelma was glad to have another boarder and Annie, Deloris, and Gracie became instant friends.

Once it was agreed that Gracie would be staying at Thelma's, she set up a time to move in and Thelma gave her a key to the front door.

"Hold on to your hat. I've got some more good news for you," Deloris said and told her about the interview at the switchboard.

Gracie was so excited that she jumped up and gave Deloris a big bear hug. Coming from such a petite young woman that should have been a challenge, but she was surprisingly strong. Deloris pulled her into the living room and drew pictures of the switchboard and all of the levers, switches and cords. She spent all afternoon teaching her everything she needed to know to be a switchboard operator.

Saturday evening, Paul didn't leave early because his buddies came to visit him at the soda fountain again. This time Walter was there, too. Deloris didn't know that he knew Paul and the brothers, but they all seemed very friendly.

Paul always acted differently—a little cocky—with the brothers there and now with Walter, he was even worse. She noticed he had taken his apron and soda jerk hat off and slipped them under the counter. Sitting with the three of them at the front table, he pretended that he was a customer instead of the soda jerk on duty. He was a jerk, all right, and here he was acting like one again. It really annoyed Deloris.

"Hey Deloris, serve us some ice cream," Paul demanded.

"Why don't you get it yourself?" she retorted.

"Come on honey. We'd rather have a pretty girl serve us rather than this ugly mug," Gordon chortled.

"No."

"You dames are all alike," Paul spoke up, getting a little irritated that she wasn't waiting on him in front of his buddies. "Do I need to talk with Mr. O'Brien about the service, or lack of it?" Gordon, George, and Walter snickered at that statement.

When he said that, Deloris relented and served them their sundaes and sodas. As she did, she turned to Walter, "What are you doing here?"

"Just having a night out with the boys," he said with a wink.

Deloris shook her head and returned to the counter. Though Paul was there, he never left his buddies, and she had to serve everyone else at the soda fountain, as well.

Annie dropped by that evening just to say hello to Deloris and get an ice cream soda, but because Gordon was staring at her and making wolf whistles the entire time, she didn't stay long. Deloris didn't blame her. George, the older brother, was okay, Deloris thought, even if he was a little arrogant. However, the younger brother, Gordon, made her nervous so she tried to not make eye contact with him. She couldn't put her finger on why she felt that way, but every time she saw him watching her, she wanted to crawl out of her skin and go hide in the back. She was glad when they all left right before closing time, even though that meant she had to clean the soda fountain by herself again.

∾

Deloris's Sunday morning shift at the switchboard went smoothly and her day got even better when, after returning home, she got a call from Leon. Leon, flirting horribly, told her he missed her and said that he'd been sent to Oklahoma City to cover an assignment for another repairman who'd been bitten by a snake. They chatted for a few more minutes until Deloris saw Gracie enter the house.

"Sorry Leon, I need to ring off. Someone just arrived that I need to talk with."

"Okay, I promise that as soon as I finish this job, I'll be back to take you on an amazing date."

Gracie was bubbling over with exhilaration. She told Deloris that she got the job so she could take the burden of her rent off her parents. Gracie told her that Mary Virginia wanted Deloris at work the next day at eight o'clock.

It was music to Deloris's ears. She could now work mornings at the switchboard and work weekends at Poppy's. Both getting what they wanted, the girls danced, hugging each other in the middle of the room. Thelma's daughters, along with Leota, came into the room to see what all the commotion was about, as did Wanda, Annie, and Thelma. When Leota heard the news, she mumbled something indiscernible and went upstairs to her room. Deloris and Gracie decided to celebrate their good news by making cookies.

Thelma gave her daughters each a cookie and sent them upstairs for a nap. Wanda retreated to her bedroom with an admonition to keep the noise down as she, too, wanted to nap.

As the cookies were passed around, Deloris said to Thelma, "Tell me more about Leota. Is she always such a wet blanket?"

Thelma shushed her sister and tried to give her a stern look, but she didn't really succeed. Gracie almost choked on a cookie at Thelma's futile attempt.

"Leota is just quiet," Thelma said in a hushed tone. "And she starts work at six in the morning as a maid at the President Hotel, which is why she takes naps in the afternoon when she's not watching the girls for me."

"What about Wanda?" Gracie asked.

"I know about Wanda," Annie said. "She's had a lot of bad things happen to her, and she's such a nice lady. Her husband died and didn't leave her anything, and her son, Terry, is just no good. A friend who lived in her old boarding house told me that she got kicked out because of Terry. He threw a fit one day when he was visiting her, and he got so angry he broke a window. Another time, he threw a chair."

"Terry doesn't visit Wanda here, and he never will," Thelma replied. "When I took her on as a boarder, I asked her for a reference from her last landlady. The landlady told me what happened, but she also said that Wanda always paid on time and had been a good boarder otherwise. So, I made Wanda promise that Terry would never come into the house or around it as a condition of renting her a room. She agreed."

"That's good," Gracie said.

Deloris shared a knowing look with Annie, but neither girl wanted to tell Thelma that Terry did come around the house even if he didn't enter it. They didn't want to cause any more problems for Wanda.

"Yes," Deloris agreed, "I wouldn't want to be around someone like her son."

"I know," said Annie. "My friend said they called him 'Terry the Terror' at the other boarding house."

The party broke up a little while later as Deloris needed to go to work at Poppy's and Gracie headed to the station to catch the evening train back home to Sedalia to pack up her things, promising she'd return in three days.

CHAPTER 17

Switchboard Friends

S unday evening when Deloris walked up to the soda fountain, she saw George and Gordon seated at a table near the big window at the front of the shop, again. Surprise, surprise. It was "their" table. This time they were hunched over it having an intense conversation. When she entered, the bell over the shop door tinkled and the two men jumped.

Paul was busy putting the clean glasses away and preparing to leave, his blue eyes looking tired and clouded. Deloris suspected that he'd stayed out late drinking and smoking with his buddies long after his shift ended the evening before. She put on her apron and started helping him.

Both George and Gordon were dressed to the nines and Deloris wondered again what they did for a living because the silk ties that they were wearing didn't come cheap. No customers were in the shop and she guessed it was because Gordon had scared them all off again.

The two got up and walked over to where she was. She

looked down intently at the soda glasses as she rinsed them, trying not to make eye contact with either of them. Paul stepped around the counter and took off his apron and cap while she was still cleaning glasses. Next time she came to work she was going to tell him that he needed to finish his whole shift before taking off, she thought to herself.

"Hey gorgeous. How about you and me going out tonight?" George asked.

"No, thanks. I have to work," Deloris replied, still looking down.

"Don't you get off at 10 p.m.? The night is still young then. We could trip the lights fantastic at Electric Park."

"I may be from the country, George. . . "

"You can call me Brown," George interrupted.

"George," she persisted. "But even I know that Electric Park closed down after a fire a few years ago," Deloris said, shaking her head. She glanced up to see that Gordon was staring at her and trying to hold her gaze, so she quickly looked down again and continued working.

"Okay, okay. You caught me. You're a real Abercrombie, you know. I've never known anyone as smart as you."

Deloris looked up at him with a puzzled look on her face.

"What? Abercrombie?" he said to answer the questioning look upon her face. "You know, Abercrombie, a real know-it-all, but I guess that I was mistaken since you didn't know that."

Deloris's face changed to pure annoyance at that comment.

"So how about we catch a movie or do some stepping out at the Pla-Mor or the Groves? I got some Jacksons burning a hole in my pocket and I need a pretty little thing like you to help me blow it."

"No, George. When I get done here, I am going straight home. I will be too tired to go dancing, partying, or to a movie."

At that, she allowed herself to look up at George and Gordon more intently. Gordon had a bandage on his neck and, come to think of it, she never saw him smile, so she couldn't check for missing teeth. Gordon usually kept his head down around Deloris; when he did say something he usually had his hand up to his mouth. She decided to ask him about the bandage.

"What happened to you?" Deloris asked.

"Oh this," he said pointing at the bandage. "I cut myself shaving," Gordon replied with a smirk and looking at the other two guys.

George snickered and said, "Yeah, Baby Face here hasn't been shaving too long and hasn't learned how to handle a razor."

Gordon turned to George and told him to shut up around the skirt, and punched him in the side. George punched him back, only harder. At that, Gordon stood up, looking for a place to land a punch as if to say, "You want to give it a go?"

Just as Deloris thought she might have to duck behind the counter if a fight broke out, the door opened and Austin came in, wearing his street clothes. When Deloris saw him, she had an idea. "Austin, it's so good to see you! How is everything at the police station?" she asked in slightly louder voice than normal. Out of the corner of her eye, she saw Paul and the other two men stiffen up.

"It's going well," Austin said, a bit confused.

"Did you make any arrests today?" she asked, keeping an eye on the three men. Gordon sat back down at the table and George quickly finished his cup of coffee. Paul looked even more nervous than usual.

"Not that many," Austin replied, catching her drift since she knew he hadn't worked that day. Austin hadn't noticed the trio when he first walked in, but saw them standing up and preparing to leave.

They had heard enough. Paul threw his cap and apron under the counter while the other two got up, and the threesome quickly left the shop. Austin watched them leave and turned to Deloris. "Okay, DeDe, what gives?"

"That was Paul, George, and Gordon. Remember from the night we followed them?"

"I thought that might be them, but I never got a close look at their mugs that evening and they left so fast tonight. Paul is the tall, skinny one with sandy hair, right?"

"You got it."

Austin smiled. "And that's why you asked all those questions, right? You wanted to see if they'd scram if a policeman came around?"

"And they scrammed like cockroaches," Deloris said with satisfaction.

"Smart move, DeDe."

"Gordon, the one with a scar on his cheek, gives me the heebie jeebies, and I've never seen him smile big enough to see his teeth."

"Do they hang out here every night?"

"Not every night, but they're pretty regular."

"If they're ever here till closing time, you call me—there's a phone here, right?"

Deloris nodded, "There's one at the main office, just outside the dressing rooms."

"You call me if they're still hanging around at closing time and I'll give you a ride home."

Austin saw the look on Deloris's face, one that he'd told her before looked remarkably similar to the stubborn face of a Missouri mule.

"I don't want anything happening to you while you're waiting for a streetcar. Plus," Austin added, "I can give Stella and Trudie a ride home, too. Do you want them to be hassled by Gordon?"

Deloris crossed her arms. "Fine. I'll call you if the Nelson brothers are ever hanging around at closing, but only for Stella and Trudie."

"Thanks, DeDe," Austin said. "You're a peach." Deloris rolled her eyes. "Tell you what," he continued, "I'll start hanging out here, too, when I get off work."

"Austin," Deloris said, changing the subject, "did you notice the bandage on Gordan's neck?"

"I did, why?"

Deloris told him she suspected that Gordon didn't really cut himself shaving. She could see scratches at the edge of the bandage. Since she couldn't check for missing teeth, she wasn't certain of their guilt yet, but Gordon mostly kept his head down when he talked, or usually had a hand close to his mouth half covering it. She certainly wouldn't put it past those two thugs to have robbed Harry and Marguerite; plus, George claimed he had money to burn. Where did he get that much money? She needed to see what the bandage was really covering up on Gordon and if he had any scratches on his arms. George too. She shivered. She didn't know how she was going to check for that, especially on Gordon.

"This all sounds good, DeDe, but there's no proof. It's totally circumstantial."

"Wait, I have an idea! I can invite George, Gordon and Paul to a swimming party at the Crystal Pool at Poppy's next weekend. That way we can see if their arms have scratches that might be from Marguerite and Tommy during the robbery."

"You don't swim. How are you going to handle that?" Austin asked, knowing that once she had her mind set on something it was useless to try and talk Deloris out of it.

"I'll figure something out before then. Are you available next Saturday afternoon? I'm afraid that Gordon or George might get a little handsy when I ask them."

Austin sighed. "I'll be there, but I don't like this one bit."

"Austin, you're the best! Just let me clean up that mess" —Deloris gestured to the table the three men had vacated, which had coffee cups and ice cream bowls full of melted remains—"and I'll make you whatever you want off the menu. It's on me."

"Before you wash their coffee cups, let me take them to the station and run their fingerprints to see if I get a match. Oh, and I'll take a mint chocolate chip cone," said Austin with a twinkle in his eye which Deloris noticed.

"Why do you want mint chocolate?"

"Because it's good at poker." Austin said.

"Why is mint chocolate ice cream good at poker?" Deloris asked, knowing that she'd regret it.

"Because," Austin said, straight-faced, "it's got all the chips."

Deloris groaned and shook her head. Then she pointed to the door, "Go. Get out of here."

After Austin left, the soda fountain got busier and busier. Everyone and their neighbor must have come to Poppy's that night. As her mother would say, she was "busier than a one-eyed cat watching two mouse holes." Luckily Mr. O'Brien stopped by to see how she was doing and started helping her with the customers. He never said anything, but it was obvious that Paul wasn't there to work his shift.

The crowd coming into the soda parlor was a mix of families, couples, and singles. With each man that came up to order something, Deloris watched their mouth to look for missing teeth and then at their hands to look for the ring. A few had missing teeth, but not in the right place. One guy was missing almost all of his front teeth, she thought he probably lost them in a fight because his nose had obviously been broken a time or two. Her bet was still on George and Gordon doing the robberies, but she had to see if Gordon had a tooth missing.

A man and woman came into the soda parlor and ordered a dollar's worth of ice cream with two malts and a sundae. The man gave Deloris a twenty-dollar bill to pay their tab. When Deloris came back with his change of nineteen dollars, he said that he changed his mind. He told her that she could just give him the twenty dollars back and he'd give her the exact change. So, she went back and retrieved the twenty, but still had the nineteen dollars in her hand. Then he said that he changed his mind again and said just take the dollar from the five dollars in his change. He needed the other change for a taxi. Then he said, "Oh, silly me. I should just give you the dollar from my change."

With the dollar in one hand and the thirty-nine dollars in the other, Deloris suddenly realized that the man was trying to shortchange her by talking about ways of changing his payment and trying to hurry her up. She had heard that there were folks going around doing that, so she stopped right there and yelled for Mr. O'Brien to come over to the table. Of all nights for this to happen with the big crowd, she thought, but luckily her boss was behind the counter. As

Mr. O'Brien came over the couple jumped up and took off, leaving all of the money with Deloris. After she explained what happened, Mr. O'Brien complimented her for catching on, and told her to take the nineteen dollars as a tip.

CHAPTER 18

Just Another Day

I t was a rainy Monday morning when Deloris took her place at the switchboard for her first weekday shift.

"What are you doing here? I thought you worked weekends?" Joyce queried.

"Yeah, what are you doing here?" Pam and Lori chimed in together.

"I found someone to work weekends, so now I work weekdays."

"Great news," they all said in unison, including Boo who had just walked in and taken her seat.

After greeting her co-workers, everyone shared what they did over the weekend and Deloris told them about the Adcock robbery.

Pam asked Deloris, "Do they have any leads?"

"No, I haven't heard any more. I told the detectives everything that I know, and I am trusting them to find the culprits." In her head she knew that she was lying, because she didn't trust Detective Timothy O'Malley—not one little bit—to work the case properly.

Then the calls started coming in: a lost purse here and a

theft there. Then Lori took a call that a dead body was found near the stoplight at Linwood and The Paseo. Joyce's board buzzed next. Someone needed an ambulance and a policeman dispatched to 14th and Broadway. Pam's buzzed next with a car theft. Boo's board buzzed with a robbery in progress at the Fidelity National Bank, at 9th and Walnut.

"Must be a Monday morning after a full moon," Pam quipped, and the other girls nodded in agreement. "People are always crazy then," she continued.

And so, Deloris's week started off with a bang when her board buzzed next with an injured person on Benton Boulevard.

By the time her shift was over, Deloris was more than ready for lunch. She headed downstairs where she met up with Austin. He introduced her to his partner, Big Jim, and then the three of them went to Myron Green's Cafeteria on Walnut to get lunch.

"I'm hungry for their broccoli and cheese soup, how about you, Austin?" Deloris said as she eyed a bowl served to the customer ahead of her.

"The fried chicken with creamed potatoes is calling my name," Austin said as he looked up the line to the area where the chicken was served.

"I'm going for the roast beef," Big Jim piped in as the line started moving again toward that section.

Once they were served and seated, Deloris asked Jim where he was from.

"Kansas City," he replied.

"You've lived here all of your life?"

"Yep."

"How long have you been a detective?"

"Six years."

"What did you do before that?"

Big Jim was trying to eat and it looked like he was starting to become annoyed with Deloris's questions, so Austin jumped in. "Big Jim was a Marine before becoming a policeman and joining the police force."

"Oh, really. That must have really prepared you for the police force.," Deloris commented.

"Yep."

"Do you have a wife or girlfriend?"

"Girlfriend."

"What's her name?"

"Edith Wellington."

"Does she work for the police department?"

"No, she teaches chemistry at Kansas City Junior College."

Deloris continued, "Oh, I know a girl who will be starting classes there in the fall. Her name is Gracie Burnett . . ."

Austin interrupted, changing the conversation because he could see that Big Jim was getting more annoyed. He brought up an armed robbery near the Sheffield Steel Plant the night before.

"That is scary," Deloris said. "What time did it happen?

Big Jim shook his head and gave Austin a warning look because he didn't think it was appropriate to talk about it in front of Deloris.

"She's okay," Austin assured him. "She has a good head for thinking through things that are puzzling and cuts to a viable solution. Besides, she'll keep asking questions about it until we tell her anyway."

Satisfied with Austin's endorsement, Big Jim answered Deloris's question, "It happened about eight o'clock in the evening."

"Do you have any suspects?" she asked.

"Nah, not yet." Big Jim answered. "The victim is in the hospital and we haven't been able to talk with him."

"He was just getting off his shift, apparently," Austin added. "Another worker found him when he came out of the building a few minutes later."

Before Deloris could ask, Austin answered, "And he didn't see anyone, but he did see a car in the distance turning at the stop sign. It was too far away to see the license, the color or any details, really."

"That is horrible," Deloris said. "My sister works near there and I worry about her. The lunch counter where she works was robbed, you know."

"Yes, we know," Austin said before taking a bite of his chicken.

"By the way, what did that Tim guy do with the information I gave you? Did he bring George and Gordon in?"

"Nah, not yet," Austin replied. "He said that he needed more to go on."

"More! Do I need to do all of his work for him?"

"Calm down," Austin tried to soothe Deloris.

"I'm sure he'll do it when the time is right," Big Jim broke in. "He's on another more urgent case right now, a murder investigation, but when he gets done, he'll go back to that one."

"Oh, hey, we did get a lead on some silver candlestick holders at a pawn shop downtown. Because O'Malley is busy with the murder case, the captain asked us to follow up on the lead. We contacted Mrs. Adcock to have her go look at them to see if they are hers," Austin added.

"Well, that is possibly some good news. We need good news this gloomy Monday," Deloris said cheerfully to lighten the mood. "When are you taking her to the pawnshop?"

"Thursday afternoon," Austin said.

"Excellent," Deloris said. "I want to go with you."

"No, DeDe, that wouldn't be appropriate."

"But . . ."

Austin gave a resounding "No."

So, Deloris changed the subject and asked Austin if he could pick up Gracie at the train station on Wednesday, since she, and all of her bags, would be arriving to move into Thelma's. Austin agreed, but told Deloris, "Someday, you need to learn how to drive a car."

"Why should I, when I have you?" Deloris replied sweetly, making Big Jim snicker.

Thursday afternoon, Austin and Big Jim went to the pawn shop to meet Marguerite Adcock. To their surprise, Deloris was standing there with her, and she explained to Austin and Big Jim that Marguerite had asked her to accompany her. By the look on his face, Austin clearly didn't believe that Marguerite had specifically asked Deloris, but he just shook his head and opened the door for the ladies to enter.

When they were inside, Big Jim showed his badge to the owner, who nervously pointed out a set of silver candlesticks on a shelf behind the counter.

"Yes, those look like mine," Marguerite said softly. "May I look at them more closely?"

"Sure thing, ma'am," the pawn shop owner said as he took the candlestick holders down from their perch.

Marguerite took one and turned it upside down. There, engraved on the bottom, was a big A.

"Yes, these are mine," Marguerite said, smiling with delight.

A silver ladle and set of silverware were displayed on the shelf below the candlesticks. The owner got those down, too, and Marguerite confirmed that they looked like her silver as well.

Big Jim stepped forward and asked the owner, "When were these items brought in and who brought them?"

The owner said, "It was sometime last week, but I need to check my book register for the exact day and who brought them in."

"How about jewelry? Did anyone bring in any jewelry lately?" Marguerite asked.

"Again, I'll check my books."

"Okay, we'll wait," Austin replied.

The owner paused a moment and then bent down, pulled up his register book, and turned to the transactions from the week before. After turning three pages with writing on both sides, he said, "Here it is. All the silver was brought in last Tuesday along with a ladies' gold wedding band and a black onyx cameo ring."

Marguerite let out a gasp of excitement. "May I see the wedding band?"

"And we need to see the black onyx ring," Austin quickly added.

"Yes, sir. I keep them down here," the pawn shop owner said as he walked to the next glass display case and bent down to unlock it. He pulled a long black box from the display that had about seventy-five or eighty gold wedding bands in it. "A lot of people have fallen on hard times lately and I've had a lot of personal items pawned," he said almost apologetically as he set the box on the counter. "I get a lot of rings. Let me know if you see yours."

Marguerite reached into the box and pulled out one of

the rings that looked a little like hers. She excitedly tried it on before looking at it closer. It was too big. With tears welling in her eyes, she took out one ring after another with no luck.

"Don't give up hope yet," Deloris encouraged her.

"Hold on there, missy. I've got another box," the owner said while reaching down to a drawer at the bottom of the display case. He pulled out a box identical to the first one containing just as many rings.

Marguerite looked and started to shake her head, when one ring caught her eye. She pulled it out of the display and put it on her finger. It fit! She took it off and looked inside where engraved in the gold were the initials HA, a heart symbol, and MR. It was definitely her ring and she was so excited to have it back.

Marguerite asked, "Do I get to take my things home?"

"Not yet," Big Jim replied gently. "We need to keep them for a while until we catch the goons who robbed you and tied you up."

"Oh yes, I understand," she said. "Do I need to stay and do anything else?"

"No, you can go. Do you want me to give you a lift home?" Austin offered.

"No, that's okay," Marguerite replied. "I have a little shopping that I need to do while I am downtown and I'll catch a bus or a streetcar home. Thank you so much for finding my belongings, officers, and thank you, Deloris, for coming with me." She then turned to the pawn shop owner and thanked him, too. She was beaming with excitement, but then a look of concern crossed her face.

"Oh, but you paid for these things. You will lose your money."

While it was true that the owner was out the money he

paid for the items, he told Marguerite that the look on her face was worth the loss.

After Marguerite left, the owner turned to Big Jim and Austin and asked, "What now?"

"We still need to see the black onyx cameo ring and get a description of the person who hawked the stolen goods," Big Jim said.

"Are there any other rings?" Deloris asked. "Ones that aren't wedding bands?"

"Right," the pawn shop owner said, bending down to put the black ring box away, and pulling out yet another ring box that was brown.

He then took a ring out of it and handed it to Austin. It matched the description of the one stolen a couple of weeks ago. "They must have hocked it right after they robbed Mrs. Adcock," Austin said.

Big Jim said, "We need to get that victim down to the pawnshop to identify the ring." He turned to the shop owner and asked, "Do you remember who pawned it?"

"I've had a lot of people in and out of my shop, so it is almost impossible to remember who brought the items in, but I will try. Let's see. The name on the items is a John Smith. Ah yes, I think I remember him: tall, slight build, a nervous guy. He was driving a Model T bucket. I saw it when I followed him to the door to lock it after he exited. It was almost closing time when he came in, you see."

"Do you remember his hair color, eye color, any distinguishing scars or marks? Anything that stands out about him?" Austin asked.

"As I said before, he was fairly tall and lanky with sandy or reddish-blonde hair. I didn't look at his eyes. That's about all I remember."

Deloris wondered if it was Paul. It certainly sounded

like his description. She vowed to ask him when she saw him at work the next night if he pawned any silver.

"Did he look like any of these guys?" Austin handed him pictures of George, Gordon, and Terry taken from their police files.

"Nah, it wasn't any of them."

"Would you mind coming down to the police station and sitting with our sketch artist to give her a description of the man?"

"Sure, but I can't leave the shop unattended. You understand. I could come by later this evening after I close or on Sunday."

"What time do you close?"

"The shop closes at five, but then I have to do paperwork. I won't be done till five-thirty."

"Come by then and I'll ask our sketch artist to wait for you."

"Okay, I'll be there at 6 o'clock."

"Thank you. We'll be in touch if we need anything else. In the meantime, if you remember anything else, give us a call," Big Jim said as he handed him a card.

"Will do, Officer."

"Do you need us to drop you off anywhere, DeDe?" Austin asked.

"No, thank you. I'll catch a bus home."

CHAPTER 19

Fired

That Friday evening, Deloris got to the park a little early so that she could talk with Paul before he left. Since the weather was a little cooler after a storm blew through earlier, the customers were few and far between. For once, Paul was alone. Good, she thought, I will be able to talk with him uninterrupted.

"Hey, Paul. How are you doing?"

"Okay."

"Where's your buddies? Aren't they usually here to meet you when you get off?"

"Yeah, but they're not coming tonight."

"Really, how come?"

"Stupid George got the chicken pox and is sick in bed and Gordon has plans."

"Oh really," Deloris said thoughtfully. To her that sealed the deal that George and Gordon must have been involved in the robbery at Marguerite's home. George must have gotten the chicken pox from Tommy. She gave a silent chuckle and thought, serves him right. She didn't need to risk her life going swimming with them to look at the scratches, now.

As Deloris walked behind the counter, she saw that Paul's jacket had fallen on the floor. Picking it up, she commented, "Is this a new jacket?"

"Yeah, my mom gave it to me for my birthday last week."

"It's a pretty dark blue color and . . ."

Before she could finish her sentence, Mr. O'Brien entered the shop, looking serious. He said hello to Deloris, and then took Paul into the back room, closing the door behind them.

Deloris started to clean the table closest to the door, but the conversation was muffled. It sounded like Paul was pleading his case about something.

Then Mr. O'Brien said something else and there was a pause. Paul jerked the door open, looked back at Mr. O'Brien, and stood there staring him in the eyes for a minute before yelling, "Great!" He threw down his cap and practically ripped his apron off before throwing it on the floor, too. When he was done with that, Paul went behind the counter, grabbing his hat and draping his new jacket over his arm.

"I'm outta here," he said angrily, glaring back at Mr. O'Brien, never looking Deloris in the eye.

Mr. O'Brien, watching him, said, "Don't forget to return that shirt before you leave."

"Yeah, yeah. You'll get it, but not tonight," Paul responded. Mr. O'Brien gave a curt nod and left the soda fountain.

"What happened?" Deloris asked. She offered him a cup of coffee, hoping to learn what the blowup had been about.

"He claims that I took some money out of the till and that I have been late three times in the last two weeks and left early. Did you rat me out?" he asked as he placed his jacket and hat down on the seat next to him.

"No, no. I haven't said anything to him or anyone. I don't even know when you arrive since your shift starts before mine, but I've been pretty upset with you for taking off early and leaving me with your messes to clean up."

"Well, someone ratted me out," Paul said, ignoring her last comment. With a wild look in his eye, he set the coffee cup down and grabbed his jacket.

He was so angry that Deloris didn't want to stir the pot and make him any angrier by asking more questions, especially about the pawn shop, so she let him storm off without a good-bye and began her shift.

After clearing off and wiping down a table, she paused. On the floor, pushed up against the base of the counter, she saw Paul's flat hat. She figured that he dropped it when he scooped up his jacket and stormed out. She decided that she would take it to him tomorrow. Maybe she could get Paul to tell her more after he'd had a chance to cool down. She'd get Austin to go with her.

Soon, the wind picked up again as another storm started to form. With the clouds looking ominous, the park emptied out fairly quickly. In fact, she realized she hadn't had a customer come in for the last hour, when Mr. O'Brien walked into the parlor again.

"I'm sorry you had to see that," he said. "I didn't realize Paul would get so angry." Deloris told him that it was all right. Mr. O'Brien looked around the empty soda fountain and told her that she could close up early because it didn't look like there was anyone else coming in that night with the storm imminent.

"Wonderful!" she said with a big smile. She decided to return Paul's hat tonight since it was still early. She closed up and locked the soda fountain and went to the office to call Austin. She asked him if he would come pick her up early and take her to Paul's house.

"He left his hat. And I have something else to tell you, too."

When Austin pulled up, Deloris got into his car. As they drove to the Sullivan house, Deloris told him about George's chicken pox.

"I can't arrest him for having chicken pox, DeDe, and it isn't even my case."

"I know, but this narrows the field of suspects, doesn't it?"

"Yes, it does do that. I can tell Detective O'Malley and see if he wants to bring him and Gordon in for questioning."

"That'd be great," she replied.

Pulling up to Paul's house, she hopped out of Austin's car and ran to the front door because she hadn't brought a jacket and she was cold. Paul's mother answered the door this time. She told Deloris that Paul wasn't home. Disappointed, Deloris gave her his hat and hurried back to the car.

When Austin and Deloris got back to Thelma's, they found a party going on. Annie was celebrating a promotion to junior reporter and Thelma had made a spread of food. They invited Austin to join, and he agreed to stay, since it was still early, and it was Friday night, after all.

Leota went upstairs after eating. Shyly shaking her mousy-brown hair, she explained that she wasn't really fond of parties. Everyone else stayed downstairs to enjoy the evening. Jazz was on the record player with Gracie keeping the music going. A game of cards was being played in the dining room and a game of dominoes tied up the coffee table in the living room. Thelma's daughters played jacks in a corner, and everyone was in a festive mood. The Davis family from next door was there, as were a few other neighbors and some of Annie's co-workers.

At 9 p.m. Wanda excused herself with a headache and went to bed. Shortly after that, Thelma shuffled the girls off to bed amid many protests and disappeared into her bedroom as well. One by one the party revelers parted ways and headed home.

Close to 10 p.m. Austin started to leave, just as Deloris realized that she had left her paycheck at the soda fountain. She asked Austin if he would mind running her over to Poppy's so she could get it.

"Can't you get it tomorrow?" he asked.

"I really need to put it in the night depository at the bank tonight. I wrote a check that will probably be at the bank tomorrow morning."

Austin shook his head at this revelation. "I could arrest you for writing bad checks, you know."

"It won't be bad if my paycheck is deposited tonight," she said innocently.

"How are you going to get in?" he asked.

"I locked up, remember? I have a key," she said holding the key up to his face.

"Okay, okay. Grab whatever you need and let's go before it gets any later. At least it looks like the storm is over."

Deloris ran to the coat closet and grabbed a rain jacket. Her purse was on the floor beside the couch and she grabbed it, too. Annie handed her a flashlight, which she readily accepted. Opening the door, she turned to Austin, "Well, come on. I'm ready."

Austin put on his hat and waved goodbye to the few folks left at the party. Because it was so late, Deloris felt safer having Austin with her. With all of the armed robberies going on, she didn't feel safe going to the park by herself. She told Austin that she remembered turning her check face down and putting it beside the cash register.

When they arrived at the back gate of the park, Deloris jumped out of the car and told Austin, "I'll only be a minute. I just need to grab the check and I'll be back in a jiffy."

"Are you sure? I could go with you to scare the boogie man away," he said sarcastically.

Deloris stuck her tongue out at him before walking quickly away, picking her route to avoid water puddles.

Holding a flashlight, Deloris walked towards to the soda fountain. The park looked ominous with its rides paused in mid-movement, with the flashlight casting wicked shadows everywhere.

As she approached the building, she noticed the flashlight revealed something in the grass on the right side of the building: a man's shoe. "That's curious," she said to no one in particular. Normally, she would have thought that a drunk passed out nearby and lost his shoe but she didn't see anyone. She walked over to it to get a closer look and flashed the light around. There behind the building, she saw a shoeless foot. Expecting to find someone completely snockered, she walked toward the foot and then stopped. She gasped when she saw that the body attached to the shoeless foot was lying face down in the mud. The person's hair and jacket were drenched from the rain.

Quickly, she turned and ran back to the car where Austin was patiently waiting.

"Did you get . . ." Austin stopped mid-sentence when he saw Deloris's face.

Breathless, she could barely get the words out. "Dead . . . body . . ."

Enough said. Austin retrieved his hat from the backseat, pulled the gun from his shoulder holster and followed Deloris to the body. She flashed the light on the body so he could see it better. Kneeling down, Austin turned the man's body over and pulled the jacket away from the face to discover that it was Paul! Deloris screamed at the revelation. She couldn't believe it. She just saw him earlier this evening and he was very much alive. She could see a small hole surrounded with blood on the chest of the white shirt from the soda fountain that he was still wearing.

Austin pulled out a handkerchief and reached over to grab a paper that was sticking out of Paul's jacket pocket. Deloris flashed the light on it so that they could both read it. The note said, "Meet me behind the Poppy's Paradise Park Soda Fountain at 10 p.m. Come alone." It was signed with only a handwritten symbol that looked like the letter "M" with the middle prong crossed like a "t".

"What do you think that means?" Deloris asked.

"The symbol must be a gang sign," Austin told her.

"I can't imagine that Paul was involved in a gang, though."

"Tuesday, our sketch artist drew a picture of the man who pawned the stolen items from your friend's house and the sketch looked like Paul. So yeah, he was probably involved in a gang. O'Malley sent an officer to pick him up for questioning, but they hadn't caught up with him yet."

"Oh," said Deloris. "So, he was in a gang with George and Gordon."

"Apparently so." Austin surmised. "I'll take you back home now and will come back tomorrow to get your statement. We don't need you to come in to the station tonight."

CHAPTER 20

The Paycheck

The next morning, as soon as Deloris woke up, she threw on her robe and went downstairs to call Poppy's Paradise Park. Mr. O'Brien answered on the third ring and told her that he'd been called in early that morning by the police. Deloris offered him her sympathies and told him about finding the body last night. Mr. O'Brien asked how she was doing, and then informed her that she didn't need to come into work—the whole park was shut down today. That was bad news for everyone who depended upon putting the hours in for their paychecks like Deloris, but was worse news for the park because the annual Associated Grocers Picnic on Thursday was in jeopardy of being cancelled. It was the biggest money maker for the park. Deloris told Mr. O'Brien she hoped the police would be done before then, and he agreed. He told Deloris he'd call all the employees as soon as he knew when the park would reopen.

After hanging up, Deloris remembered why she'd gone to the park the night before. "Oh my gosh, I forgot to go to the night drop box with my check last night! Oh no. I forgot to get my check!" Deloris cried out to no one. In a panic, she ran back up the stairs to her bedroom.

Annie knocked on Deloris's door. "Are you awake? I thought I heard you say something. Can I come in?"

"Yes, yes. Come in," Deloris almost shouted as she rushed around her bedroom trying to get dressed as fast as she could.

Watching her mad dash around the room, Annie asked, "What's the matter?"

"I forgot to get my paycheck last night and go to the bank. Oh, because I found a dead body last night at the park."

"What?!"

"When I went to the park to get my paycheck, I found Paul Sullivan's dead body behind the building. But I don't have time to fill you in on the details. Right now, I need to get my paycheck."

"Can't you get it later?"

"No, I wrote a check and I need those funds in the bank today before noon to cover it," Deloris said anxiously.

"Relax, we can go get the check as soon as you get ready and you can fill me on the details. Thelma left some cooked sausage on the table for you."

"I don't know if I can get the check or not. The soda fountain is closed while the police investigate and I don't know if they will let me in to get my check."

"Maybe you can ask Austin to get it for you, or I can try using my newspaper pass?" Annie suggested.

"Good idea." Deloris ran to the bathroom to finish getting ready. Meanwhile, Annie went downstairs and wrote a note to tell Thelma where they had gone, then called a taxi.

Deloris came downstairs in a flurry, ran to the kitchen, and grabbed the sausage and a gulp of lukewarm coffee.

Annie called from the living room that the taxi had arrived and the girls rushed out the door. Deloris had to run back inside to grab her purse, but then they were off.

At Poppy's Paradise Park there were police cars everywhere and two policemen standing guard at the entrance. As they exited the taxi, Annie asked the driver to wait for their return. They ran up to the entrance.

"Sorry, miss, but the park is closed today," one of the officers informed Deloris as he raised his hand in a stop motion.

"Oh yes, I know. I need to talk with either Detective Austin Martin or Detective Jim Anderson. It is very important that I speak with one of them," Deloris said urgently.

"I'm sorry miss, but they're both busy. We had a murder here last night."

"I know. I'm the one who found the body," Deloris said as she looked down, disappointed.

"Why didn't you say so? I suspect they need to talk with you. Wait here while I go get one of them." When he left, the other officer standing guard moved in front of the girls to prevent them following him.

Annie sidled up to the remaining officer and started asking him questions as she pulled a notepad and pen out of her purse, "So I'm a reporter with the *Kansas City Post.* What can you tell me about this case?" she asked, flashing her press pass.

"Sorry, miss. I'm not at liberty to say anything about this investigation."

The other officer returned at this point with Austin following him.

"DeDe, what are you doing here? I told you that I

would talk with you later," Austin said, making the officer look at Deloris suspiciously.

"I know," Deloris said, taking Austin's arm and leading him out of the earshot of the officers. "Austin, I forgot to get my paycheck last night in all the commotion and as I told you last night, I need it as soon as possible."

"Oh yes, I completely forgot about that. Where is it?

"It's face down at the side of the cash register."

"Okay, let me see what I can do. Please wait over there with Annie."

"Yes, I'll go over there and wait," Deloris replied as she looked impatiently at her watch. She didn't have much time before the bank closed at noon.

A few minutes later, Austin returned with the check much to Deloris's relief. "Here you go."

"Thank you so very much. You are a lifesaver."

"I'll come by the house later, after we get everything processed here."

"Okay, I'll see you then."

The young officers at the gate looked a little puzzled, but both smirked at Austin. Deloris could tell that they were thinking she and Austin might have something going on, which repulsed her. Since she and Austin had grown up together, he was more like another brother to her. As she and Annie turned quickly and walked away, she could hear Austin say, "What are you looking at? She's like my sister. Wipe those grins off your faces."

"Yes, sir."

The taxi had waited for their return as they requested and Deloris and Annie headed to the bank. It was going to cost a little extra for the taxi but, it was worth it to beat the twelve-noon closing.

After making the deposit at eleven forty-five, Deloris

and Annie caught a bus and went home to eat lunch and discuss the events of the past twenty-four hours.

"When we get home, do you mind if I hang around to listen to your story when you tell Thelma and then when Austin comes later to hear what he has to say?" Annie asked.

"No, I don't mind at all," Deloris approved. "I'm anxious to hear what he had to say as well."

CHAPTER 21

The Symbol

Once home, Deloris and Annie met Thelma at the door as she returned from the grocery store. Deloris looked around the living room and asked, "Say, where is everybody?"

"Leota took the girls to the park to play," Thelma replied. "Gracie, as you know, is working the switchboard today, and Wanda said that she'd be out most of the day visiting her son."

Deloris started filling Thelma in about what had happened the night before and Annie listened. She gave an abbreviated version to spare her some of the gory details.

"How are you doing?" Thelma asked with concerned.

"Oh, I'm all right, but it was a great shock."

"I know it was. I mean, I can't imagine how I would feel if I found a dead body," Thelma said. "Can I get you something to eat or drink?"

"No, I'm okay, thank you, but could you help me get some food together to take to Mrs. Sullivan?"

Thelma readily agreed. "I'll go ahead and start fixing

some things now," Thelma offered and went into the kitchen.

"Thank you," Deloris called after her.

Annie turned to Deloris and said, "I am so sorry that you had to go through that. Do you want to talk more about it?"

"Well, I suppose it can't hurt to go over things again to keep it all straight in my head," Deloris replied.

In the middle of relating what happened, she suddenly stopped, realizing a detail she had forgotten before. The note! The symbol on the note was one she had seen before—but where? She searched her memories. Oh yes, Gordon had shown Paul a note that had the symbol on it! So, Paul really was involved in a gang. She shook her head in sadness at that thought and what it got him.

Annie looked puzzled at her sudden silence, but as she had learned in reporting, she waited for Deloris to continue her story.

"Oh, sorry. I just remembered something else."

She told Annie about the symbol, and drew it out to show her. Annie promised to research it and see what she could find out.

"Look," Annie said, "I know the crime reporter would love to talk with you when I submit my story to him."

"Maybe later. I need to give my statement to Austin first and tell him about this revelation before I talk to the newspaper. I suspect they will want you to hold off on reporting anything about the symbol."

"Okay. I understand, but I'm going to call him and at least give him a heads up."

At that, Annie excused herself and went to the phone to call her boss. She told him that she had a big story about a murder at Poppy's Paradise Park developing and would fill him in later. She was still gathering facts. He told her that he would let her have the byline and it would be in the Sunday paper if she could get the story to him by 10 p.m. that night. Excited at the opportunity, Annie relayed the news to Deloris, who was in the kitchen with Thelma.

~

Austin said that he would come around that afternoon and ask Deloris a few more questions, but the day was dragging on and he hadn't shown up yet. She was starting to wonder what happened to him. About three o'clock he finally knocked on the front door and she ran to open it.

"Hello, Deloris."

"Oh, so formal, Austin. What's wrong? Are you mad at me or something?"

"No, no. I'm just a little tired. It's been an exhausting day."

"I'm sorry. Here, have a seat. Can I get you something to drink or eat?"

"A Coke would be nice," Austin said with a weak smile.

"Thank you again for getting my check. We made it to the bank just in time. By the way, what have you learned so far?"

"You know I can't divulge what we have learned."

Deloris sighed, "I figured you would say that. Well, I remembered something that might help you. I saw Gordon showing a note to Paul with the same symbol on it when I served them coffee last week. I drew it here for Annie to see and she is going to see what she can find out about it," Deloris said, nodding to Annie who was sitting nearby. She looked up from writing and smiled.

"That can actually help us quite a bit. I've got an officer

trying to track it down, but he hasn't had any luck yet. Annie, let me know what you find out."

"Roger," Annie replied with a slight salute. "I don't know why I did that," she said, giggling. "It was just that you said it like an order and I felt a salute was needed."

"Oh, I'm sorry," Austin said. "I didn't intend to sound like that."

"It's okay. I'm just happy to be able to help in some way."

"Okay, let's get down to business, DeDe," Austin said, taking out his notepad and pen.

"Okay," Deloris replied, sitting up a little straighter in her chair.

"What can you tell me about the last time you saw Paul?"

"Well, it was just last night, as you know."

"Alive, DeDe. Alive."

"Yes, yes, but it was last night. I saw him arguing with our manager, Mr. O'Brien, when I arrived to work. Paul left in a huff and stormed out dropping his cap."

"Did he and Mr. O'Brien have many arguments?"

"No, not that I ever saw. This was the first time. Paul could get away with just about anything at work. They were related and had an Irish comradery, a brotherhood, so to speak. Mr. O'Brien really liked Paul."

"I see. What sort of things did Paul get away with?"

"He almost always left early, leaving me to clean up after him. I was getting angry with him and planned to tell him to stop it when I got there last night. Plus, I was going to ask him about fencing the jewelry, but because of the argument he had with Mr. O'Brien, I didn't."

"I don't want you asking suspects questions before us,

DeDe," Austin admonished. Then he continued, "Have you seen him argue with anyone else?"

"No, but I know that he and Wanda's son, Terry, used to be friends, but when George and Gordon were around Paul acted like he didn't want to be around Terry. That's what Wanda told me. Remember Paul was with George and Gordon when they beat Terry up that night at the dairy."

"That's right. We'll be bringing Terry in for questioning as well as George and Gordon."

"I'd like to be a fly on the wall when you question them," Deloris said with a wink.

"No, you know you can't."

"Oh, I know. When do you think you will allow Poppy's to reopen?"

"We should be finished processing it by tomorrow or Monday at the latest."

"Wow."

"Why?" Austin asked.

"We have the annual Associated Grocers picnic on Thursday and we have some prep work planned to do this weekend. If the park is closed for too long, we won't be ready."

"I see. We should be done by tomorrow, but I'll tell the captain and we'll try to wrap it up as quickly as we can."

"Thank you. I'm sure Mr. O'Brien will appreciate that, as will the rest of us who need our paychecks to have all the hours on them."

"Happy to help. Well, I think that's all the questions I have. I'd better be off."

"Hey Austin, before you go, can you drop me off at Paul's mother's house?"

"Why do you want to go there?" Austin asked suspiciously.

"I wanted to take her some food and express our condolences over the loss of her son."

"I suppose I could do that, but I'm coming with you. I planned to talk with her anyway but I was waiting until tomorrow."

"Me, too," Annie said jumping up from the table. "I want to come, too."

"Wow, we will be quite the entourage. I suppose it's okay," Austin said, smiling as she went into the kitchen to help Thelma finish getting the food ready and packed up.

CHAPTER 22
Mary Margaret

At the Sullivan house, Deloris knocked on the door and Paul's sister answered. From another room his mother yelled, "Who is it, Mary Margaret?"

She yelled back, "It's the lady who brought Paul's paycheck the other day."

"Oh, all right, dear," Paul's mother said and walked up behind Mary Margaret. Surprised at seeing more than Deloris at the door, she said, "Won't you come in?"

As she sat down in the living room, she motioned for Deloris and her entourage to have seats on the sofa. Her face was blotchy and her eyes were red from crying. Two younger children came in and clung to her. Mary Margaret watched her mother like a German shepherd dog watches its master for the next command, ready to pounce, protect, and defend.

Deloris began, "Mrs. Sullivan, we are so very sorry for your loss. My sister made this casserole for you and the children. She also sent along this care package of light rolls, bread, milk, eggs, cookies, and a peach cobbler."

At that, Annie raised up the box that she was carrying

and Mary Margaret leaped into action. She took the casserole and told her younger brother and sister to take some of the things out of the box and follow her. Then the trio returned to gather the remaining items.

"How are you doing? I know this must have been a great shock to you," Deloris continued.

"Yes, I . . ." she stopped talking and started crying.

"I understand," Deloris said as she rose from the sofa, stepped forward, and leaned over to put her arms around Mrs. Sullivan. Paul's mother readily accepted the act of kindness. Austin offered her his handkerchief.

Mrs. Sullivan continued, "I warned Paul that hanging around those boys would get him into trouble, but he insisted that they weren't that bad, just misunderstood."

Annie chimed in, "Is there anything we can do for you?" and Deloris nodded her head in agreement. Austin sat quietly observing.

"No," Mrs. Sullivan paused in replying. "Thank you. We'll get by somehow." She started crying again softly and covered her face with the handkerchief.

For once, Deloris didn't know what to say.

At this point Austin spoke up, "Mrs. Sullivan, my name is Austin Martin, and I am a detective with the Kansas City, Missouri Police Department. We are very sorry for your loss, too. We want to catch the person who did this as soon as possible. Would it be all right if I come by later to ask you a few questions and search Paul's room?"

Mrs. Sullivan looked first at him and then at Deloris and Annie. The children had returned to the living room at this point as well.

"Oh, yes, yes. I suppose you do have questions. Why come back? Now is as good as later."

"Are you sure? I could just as easily come back with a search warrant," Austin offered.

"No, I already have family coming tomorrow, and now they will be staying for a while longer for the funeral. This is probably the better time. Do you want to talk here or in the kitchen?"

"Wherever is more comfortable to you,"

"We can go into the kitchen and I will put on a pot of coffee." She rose from her seat and walked into the kitchen.

Austin followed her as did Deloris and Annie, but he stopped at the door and waved them back. Deloris started to protest but looked at the children's faces and decided that she and Annie would be better at helping with them.

Turning toward Mary Margaret she asked, "So, what grade are you in at school?"

"I was in the seventh grade at E. F. Swinney Elementary."

"Was?" Deloris queried.

"Yes, school is out for the summer and hasn't started this year yet."

"Oh yes, silly me. When does school start?" Deloris asked, continuing with the small talk while Annie played with the two younger children.

"Well, it starts in August, but I'm not sure that I will be going back." Mary Margaret said wistfully.

"Oh?" Deloris didn't know how to respond to that.

"Paul and Mama took turns staying with my brother and sister while I went to school last year, but now . . ." Mary Margaret started crying and Deloris took her into her arms and hugged her. Deloris hadn't allowed herself to cry yet and the younger girl's sadness caused the tears to well up in her eyes, too.

"I know, sweetheart, I know. We will both miss Paul."

Mary Margaret stood back a moment and said, "You worked with my brother, right?"

"Yes, I did."

"Did you see him yesterday?"

Deloris didn't think that it was her place to tell Mary Margaret or her mother that Paul was fired yesterday or that she found his body last night, so she just said, "Yes."

"Did he say anything to you about buying a doll?"

"No, I don't believe he did. Why?"

"Well, tomorrow is my sister's birthday and he was supposed to buy a Kewpie doll for us to give to her."

Deloris looked at Annie who overheard and shook her head in sadness. Deloris hugged Mary Margaret a little closer.

Austin and Mrs. Sullivan walked into the living room at that time and Austin asked, "Which room was Paul's?"

Mrs. Sullivan pointed up the stairs and said, "Last door on the right." She reclaimed her seat in the overstuffed chair and two young children climbed onto her lap and Mary Margaret sat on the floor at her feet.

"Were you planning a party this weekend?" Annie asked, pointing at a handful of homemade decorations on the side table next to the sofa.

"Yes, they are for Catherine's fourth birthday." She looked down at the little girl and gave her a hug. "That's why we were having family coming over tomorrow. Now..."

Deloris took the opportunity of Mrs. Sullivan's pause to change the subject and ask her about the symbol. She took the picture she had drawn when explaining it to Annie out of her purse. "Do you know what this symbol is, or recognize it?"

"No," she answered, shaking her head. "The detective asked me the same question."

Mary Margaret spoke up and said, "Yes," surprising everyone. "I saw it on something in Paul's room," she offered.

"What were you doing in Paul's room? I told you about going in there," her mother admonished.

Lowering her head she said, "I'm sorry, Mama. I just went in to borrow a pencil for school. Paul always gave me a pencil when I needed a new one and he had already left when I discovered I didn't have one."

Deloris interrupted, "What did you see it on?"

"It was just a note that said, 'Meet at regular meeting place, 10 p.m.' Honest, Mama, I didn't intend to snoop. The note was laying there open."

Turning toward Mrs. Sullivan, Deloris asked, "Do you know who Paul was meeting? Did Paul have a secret girlfriend or was Paul in a gang?"

"Not that I knew anything about. Didn't he say anything to you at the soda fountain?"

"I know that he ran around with George and Gordon Nelson and sometimes Terry Phillips." Deloris added his name to see what Mrs. Sullivan's reaction would be.

"Oh, Terry. Yes, he and Paul used to be friends in school. I wish Paul didn't run around with the Nelson boys. They are bad news, but he is—," she paused and corrected, "was an adult and I couldn't stop him."

Then Austin came downstairs and thanked Mrs. Sullivan for allowing him to search Paul's bedroom and answering his questions. Deloris noticed that his suit jacket pockets now had something in them, but she didn't say anything.

"I hope it helps you to catch whomever did this to my son," Mrs. Sullivan said, and started crying again as she walked the trio to the door.

Deloris stopped her and said, "Remember, if you need anything just let me know. Here is my phone number. I'll come back next week for the dishes and milk bottle."

Austin added, "And here is my number. If you think of anything else, please give *me* a call." At this he gave Deloris a stern look.

As they piled into Austin's car, Deloris asked him to take them to the five-and-dime store.

"Why?"

"I'll explain on the way."

CHAPTER 23
Surprises and Facts

An hour later, Austin returned with Deloris and Annie to Mrs. Sullivan's house. Again, Mary Margaret answered the door, and Deloris handed her a bag. Mary Margaret looked inside to see a wrapped gift with a blank card on top. When she realized what it was, she sat the gift inside the door and stepped back outside to give Deloris a big hug, tears streaming down her face. Annie then stepped forward and handed her a box with a birthday cake inside.

"Oh, thank you. Thank you. This will help my mama too."

She held the cake with her left hand and gave Annie a hug, then waved to Austin in the car. She turned and ran inside with the cake yelling, "Mama!" When she came back to the door, Deloris and Annie had already started walking away.

Before the girls could get back to the car, Mrs. Sullivan came running outside to catch them and give them each a big hug. She then ran to the driver's side of the car and Austin stepped out of the car when he saw her coming. She threw her arms around him, too. With a look of surprise, he gave her a little hug back before she returned to the house.

As Austin pulled the car away from the curb, they waved to the family of four who stood at their stoop waving back with smiles and tears all around.

"Doesn't that just make your heart so happy?" Annie piped up, breaking the silence in the car and all agreed. Deloris noticed that even Austin had a sniffle or two from the experience.

"All right. Let's compare notes. Okay, Austin?" Deloris asked.

"Not sure what I can share with you."

"Oh, come on. You wouldn't have had the opportunity you had this afternoon, if it wasn't for me—us," she corrected, looking at Annie.

"Okay, okay." Austin said.

"We can go back to Thelma's and swap information."

"I need to go to the station first, but I'll come by afterwards."

"And I need to go to the newspaper to type all of this up, now that I have most of the lowdown on the story," Annie declared.

By the time Annie and Austin returned to Thelma's, supper was on the table. Seeing Austin, Thelma invited him to sit down and eat with them. Having not eaten since a light breakfast and very seldom being offered home cooking, he readily accepted.

Suppertime was when everyone sat around the table and shared what happened during their day. Deloris had already told the other boarders an abbreviated version of what happened the night before, so Gracie went first and regaled everyone with her experiences on the weekend switchboard. Leota listened quietly and Wanda asked Gracie a few questions about some of the emergencies and how she felt dealing with them.

"It can get rough at times," she answered. "You want to help but realize the best help you can give is getting others there as quickly as possible."

Deloris said sadly, "Sometimes there is nothing you can do to help them." She then told everyone else about finding the body the night before, and everyone at the table grew quiet.

Wanda was the first to break the silence. "Deloris, I am so sorry you had that experience. It must have been frightening."

Everyone turned to Deloris in anticipation of her answer. "It is nothing I want to ever repeat," she said. "It was scary and sad."

Wanda continued, "Was it a man or a woman?"

"I worked with him. His name was Paul Sullivan."

Wanda gasped, "Oh my goodness. Not Paul? That can't be?" Regaining her composure she looked at Deloris and said, "He, he was my son's best friend. I am in shock. He was such a nice young man."

"I know. I was in shock, too. Tomorrow is his little sister's birthday and he was supposed to bring her a doll for a present. That had us all crying. We took the casserole to his family along with your care package, Thelma. They were very appreciative of your thoughtfulness. Then we went shopping and bought the little girl a doll and a cake. It was very touching."

After the meal, everyone except Leota and Wanda pitched in to clear the table and clean the kitchen. Leota

JULIET E. SIDONIE

had to go feed her cat and Wanda said that she needed to take some new medicine that she had picked up at the Katz Drug Store earlier. Deloris sent Thelma off to take a nap, and the trio of Austin, Annie, and Deloris sat back down at the kitchen table to talk.

"Okay, you first," Deloris encouraged Austin. "What did you take out of Paul's room and hide in your suit pockets?"

"Well, I found a few notes in the trash with the same handwritten symbol on them mostly talking about meeting somewhere or another. It is obviously a gang symbol—one I've never seen or heard of before. I found a gun hidden in a box in the top of his wardrobe and a Bowie knife hidden in the slats of his bed. Since we didn't find any weapons on the body, I assume he was meeting a friend, not planning on defending himself. So, tomorrow Big Jim and I will interrogate the Nelsons and Terry Phillips."

Just then, Wanda walked into the kitchen and said that she was there for a glass of water to take her pills. Everyone stopped talking while she was there and resumed once she left.

"Okay, your turn," Austin said turning toward Deloris.

"Yes, well, I guess I don't have anything new to add to that, really. Mary Margaret saw a note on Paul's desk saying something about meeting at the regular place. Mrs. Sullivan wasn't too keen on Paul running around with George and Gordon."

"I should have the preliminary autopsy report first thing Monday morning, and when we round up his friends, we'll see what they have to say or add. Right now, it's getting late and I need to go home and get some rest," Austin said as he stood, yawned, and stretched.

"I'll let you know what I find out about the symbol as

soon as I know anything," Annie added, and the pals said goodnight.

On Monday, Deloris got up early. She wanted to get to the police station before her shift started to see if Austin had any updates. When she got there, another woman was walking towards Austin's desk, and Deloris caught up with her. Curious as to who she was, Deloris introduced herself, "Hi, my name is Deloris Markham and I work here. What's yours?"

"Carolyn Bechtel."

"What do you do here?"

"I'm the assistant coroner."

They stopped at Austin and Big Jim's desks. Austin looked up, smiling widely when he saw Carolyn. Then he groaned when he noticed Deloris standing slightly behind her.

"Good morning," Carolyn said with a fresh and inspiring attitude. "I have the preliminary results from the Sullivan autopsy." She had a folder in her hand and paused, unsure whether to hand it to Big Jim or Austin. Big Jim reached for it, so she handed it to him. As he was reading the file, she turned to Austin and started to tell him what she discovered, but she stopped, looking at Deloris.

Austin waved his hand and said, "It's all right. She'll find this out one way or another anyway."

Satisfied, Carolyn imparted her findings. "He died sometime between 10 p.m. and 2 a.m. The weapon was most likely an older revolver because it is a different size bullet than the ones used today. The bullet entered his back, nicked the aorta, and exited straight through his chest. He bled out pretty quickly."

"So, he was shot in the back? The killer couldn't even face him. Excellent work, Miss Bechtel," Austin praised. "I suspect he was killed shortly after 10 p.m. because the note in his pocket was for a meeting at 10 and we found the body about 10:30."

"That means that the murderer may have been close by when you two arrived," Big Jim noted.

Carolyn nodded, and asked, "Will there be anything else?" Big Jim shook his head and looked at Austin, but Austin seemed to be lost in thought, gazing off into space in a direction which happened to be in line with where Miss Bechtel was standing. She stood there for a moment or two, expecting him to say something else. When he didn't, she said, "Well, I have nothing further to add, so I will return to my lab."

"Oh yes, sorry. My mind wandered off for a moment there. Thank you, Miss Bechtel," Austin replied and Big Jim echoed his thanks.

"You can call me Carolyn, Detective Martin."

"Oh, yes, and you may call me Austin, Miss, er, uh, Carolyn." Deloris noticed that Austin blushed and seemed a little flustered as the assistant coroner turned and walked away.

Captain Denton walked up to Austin and Big Jim and said, "Hey, they just brought in those two guys you wanted to interrogate."

"The Nelson brothers?" Big Jim asked.

"Yeah, I think so," he replied, then went into his office.

"Sorry, DeDe, time for you to head up to the switch-board, we've got to go talk to the brothers."

"Sure, but could we meet for lunch?"

"I don't know. I'll let you know later."

Deloris looked at Austin for a second, and then smiled sweetly. "Okay."

She had another plan in mind as she headed up the stairs to the switchboard. When she got there, she still had about ten minutes before her shift started, and luckily Mary Virginia was already in her office. Deloris told Mary Virginia that she needed to go back downstairs and answer a few more questions about the dead body she found. She'd only be about twenty or thirty minutes, maybe a little longer.

Mary Virginia agreed to let her leave. After waiting a minute or two to allow time for Austin and Big Jim to go into the interrogation room so they wouldn't see her, Deloris went down the back stairs. Coming from the front of the station, she could hear a din of yelling and cursing from people who had been arrested and brought to the front desk, but thankfully the interrogation rooms and restrooms were in the back where it was quieter. Deloris looked around to make sure no one saw her before slipping into the ladies' restroom.

CHAPTER 24

The Nelsons

Once inside the restroom, Deloris carefully checked to ensure she was alone. Then, she went into a stall that was the closest to the vent where she had heard voices before. She stood up on the stool to get closer to the vent. From her perch, Deloris heard Austin ask, "Your name is George Nelson, correct?

"Yes."

"Where do you live?"

"I live at 3411 East 8th Street."

"And you knew Paul Sullivan, correct?"

"Yes."

"How did you know Paul Sullivan?"

"We went to school together."

"Okay, When did you last see Mr. Paul Sullivan?"

"I've been sick the last three days, so I don't know—maybe Wednesday or Thursday."

"Where were you Friday night about 10 p.m.?"

"Well, as I just said, I've been sick so I was at home in bed," George said with a touch of insolence.

"What can you tell me about this symbol?" Big Jim asked.

"I don't know anything about it," George replied, but he sounded wary.

"Come now, George. You're telling me that you have never seen this symbol before?"

"Nah."

"We have a witness who says they saw you in Paul's company when a note with the symbol on it was given to him."

"It wasn't me."

"Fine." Austin sounded frustrated. He opened the door and told someone, probably a guard, to return George to his cell, and to bring up Gordon. Once George had left, Big Jim told Austin, "Let me try to talk to him; you pay attention and see if he flinches when you bring up the symbol."

"Got it," Austin replied, and after a minute, Deloris heard the door open again.

"Hey, can I get some smokes?" Gordon asked as soon as he entered the room, sounding cool, calm and collected.

"Sit down," Big Jim's voice boomed. "You can get some smokes if you cooperate and answer my questions. Your name is Charles Gordon Nelson, correct?"

"I don't know, is it?"

"Okay wise guy. Do I need to get tough with you? Answer the question," Big Jim said sternly.

"You say it is, but I go by Gordon."

"All right, Gordon. Where do you live?"

"I live here, I live there. I live here and there."

"Do you understand me, boy? This is serious. You are a suspect in a murder case. Right now, I could hold you for insubordinate behavior toward an officer of the law." Big

Jim's voice rose, and he sounded like a drill sergeant as he shouted.

Deloris had never heard of that offense before. She imagined that Big Jim was hovering over Gordon and giving him the intimidating look that she'd heard Austin describe.

"Listen, you can make this easy or we can do it the hard way. The sooner you cooperate, the sooner you get the smokes. Got it?"

There was a pause, and then Gordon said, "Yes, sir... But, can I get a Coke?"

"When we finish these questions."

"But I'm thirsty now."

"Then you better hurry up and answer my questions."

"Yes, sir."

"All right," Big Jim said. "Where do you live?"

"I occasionally live at 3411 East 8th Street, Kansas City, Missouri, with my brother."

"What does that mean, 'occasionally'?"

"I live there when I ain't in jail."

"Okay. Better. You are an acquaintance of Paul Sullivan, correct?"

"Yeah, I knew him."

"How well did you know Mr. Sullivan?"

"Uh, Paul. Yeah. He was my brother's friend, but we hung out sometimes."

"Okay. When was the last time you saw Paul?"

"Oh, uh. I don't know. Maybe last Thursday. Yeah, yeah, last Thursday."

"Okay, where were you Friday night about 10 p.m.?"

"Uh, I was at a party with some friends. Yeah, that's right. I was at a party that night."

"Was Paul at this party?"

"No, no. He had to work."

"We have a witness that said he left work about 4 p.m."

"Oh, uh, yeah, yeah. I remember now. He was at the party for a while, but he was mad and he left early when a bunch of your goons came and tried to break-up the party."

"Why was he mad?"

"He lost his job."

"You said a bunch of police officers came and tried to break-up the party? Why?"

"Someone called that we were too noisy, so we quieted down and continued."

"Where was the party? Who was the host?"

"It was at Mac's place."

"Who is Mac?"

"Mac? Hmm, let me see. I think his name is McKinley. Yeah, yeah Walt McKinley."

"Where does this McKinley live?"

"I don't know the exact address, somewhere around 24th and Lawn."

"I see. How many people were at the party?"

"Maybe fifteen or sixteen?"

"Was your brother at the party?"

"Nah, my brother was at home sick with the chicken pox. I didn't want to get them, so I've been staying away from him."

"Can you give me the names of any other people at the party? To verify your alibi."

"Mac can give you a better idea of who all was there."

"We'll ask him later. I need to hear it from you now."

"Okay, okay. Uh, Terry. Yeah, yeah, Terry Phillips was there with his girlfriend and, uh, Terry's mom stopped by at the beginning but only for a moment. She was trying to get him to leave with her, but he wouldn't go. He's such a momma's boy," Gordon chuckled.

"Anyone else?" Big Jim pressed.

"Well, there was a babe there that I was making time with, but I only got a first name—Betty Sue. We connected, if you know what I mean," Gordon said smugly, "and I went back to her place."

"Where does she live?"

"Well, I was feeling the hooch and can't say exactly— somewhere on Benton Boulevard, I think."

"All right. Can you describe Betty Sue?"

"Well, yeah she had big headlights . . ." Gordon's voice drifted off dreamily.

"What else?" Big Jim asked, bringing Gordon back to reality.

"I didn't see much else."

"Come on, lover boy. You can give me a better description than that."

Gordon finally surrendered to Big Jim's questions. "Okay. She had blonde hair like Jean Harlow."

"How tall was she?"

"Oh, I don't know, about this high."

"All right. Now we're getting somewhere. Have you seen this symbol before?" Big Jim interjected suddenly. He must be trying to catch Gordon off guard, Deloris thought.

"Nah, I ain't seen that before. What is it?"

"That's what we are trying to find out."

"Oh, it looks kind of funny, like an upside-down pitch-fork, don't it?"

"Yeah, well you don't recognize it at all? I thought it looked like you did."

"Nah, I just thought it looked funny was all. Can I have that Coke now?"

"I'll tell the officer outside to bring you one in the cell."

"You mean I can't go?"

"No, we may have some more questions later. I'm sending you back to the holding cell."

"Why? I answered all of your questions. What about my smokes?"

"Oh yeah." Deloris heard what she assumed was Big Jim hitting a pack of cigarettes against his hand to get one to pop up and then he must have handed it to Gordon. "Here."

Austin called for the guard to come and take Gordon back to his cell. Once Gordon was gone, Big Jim said, "Come on, let's go compare notes," and the two detectives left the room.

After everything was quiet, Deloris opened the restroom door a crack and looked out to ensure that no one was around. Then she started to walk down the hall to the room where the detectives' desks were, but she ran into Austin and Big Jim on the way.

"What are you doing here? Aren't you supposed to be working? Have you been down here all this time?" Austin asked suspiciously.

"No, silly. I went to work, but the bathroom upstairs was occupied, so I came down here to use this one. I just got down here a moment ago," she answered innocently. "Also, I wanted to ask if we are on for lunch today? How about Green's Cafeteria?"

Satisfied with her answer, Austin replied, "Sounds good to me." And Big Jim nodded his head.

"Okay, I'll see you soon. By the way, did you learn anything from George or Gordon?" Deloris slipped in, trying to catch Austin off-guard.

"Nothing we can tell you," he answered curtly.

"You know that I can help you. Why don't you let me try?"

"Because we could get into trouble with the captain if

he found out we were talking about the case to anyone outside of the station."

"I'm inside the station," she smiled craftily, then turned and went back upstairs.

"Sorry, I'm a little late. It took me a little longer than I expected," Deloris told Mary Virginia when she reported back to work.

"That's all right Deloris. It has been moderately quiet up here and you were only gone for thirty minutes."

"That's good to hear."

When she took her seat, Pam turned and asked, "Where were you?"

"I had some business downstairs to attend to."

From then on, the board remained relatively slow. Once her shift was over, she grabbed her things and headed back downstairs.

"Hey, are you guys ready?" she asked as she approached Austin's desk.

"Sure, I just need to type this last part and I'll be done with my report." He typed a few more words with his index fingers and pulled the paper and its carbon copy out of the typewriter. He signed the bottom and stepped inside Captain Denton's office to put the original in the inbox on his desk. The captain looked up from talking on the phone and waved at Austin in acceptance.

"Let's get out of here," he said as he grabbed his hat and Big Jim did the same. "Shall we walk to the cafeteria?"

"That's fine with me," Deloris replied.

They exited the station and started walking down the street.

Once they had their food, Deloris said, "I saw the Nelsons escorted out of the interrogation room this morning."

"Oh really," Austin replied indifferently.

"Come on, dish the dirt on them," Deloris implored. "You know I won't stop until you tell me something."

"No, DeDe."

"I can help you, remember?"

"Okay, okay," Big Jim surprised her as the first to crack from her pleading. "I don't think the brothers killed Paul."

Austin looked at him incredulously. "What are you doing telling her this?"

"What? I was certain..." Deloris paused.

"I know. We were certain, too. However, I do believe they had something to do with the robberies in the more affluent neighborhoods and possibly robbed your friends, the Adcocks."

"Really. Well, that doesn't surprise me at all."

At that moment, Annie walked in.

"Annie! How did you find us here?" Deloris and Austin said in unison.

"I'm an investigative reporter, remember. I can find people and things," she answered confidently. They all looked at her, amused. "Oh, all right, I went by the station and they told me that you guys were going to lunch. I left a message and started walking to the bus stop when I saw all of you through the window."

"Great. Well pull up a seat and join us," Austin offered.

"Thanks, I will," she answered, and Austin introduced her to Big Jim. After she gave her order, she turned to Austin and said, "I've got some news to tell you. I cracked the symbol information."

After hearing the desired gasp from all three of them,

she continued, "Flash! News bulletin! It is an ancient Celtic symbol."

"Celtic? Oh, yeah, yeah. Irish."

"Well, yes, or basically the United Kingdom. Anyway, it is the symbol used for one of the old Irish mobs," Annie said triumphantly. "The symbol is the Malbon and they called themselves the Malbon Gang. They used the Celtic symbol to identify each other by a tattoo on their right foot."

"You're using past tense," Deloris noted. "Do they still exist?"

"Well, no one has heard of them for about thirty or forty years. It was thought that they were no longer around—until now, of course," Annie added.

"Are you on the up and up? How did you find this out? Never mind, I don't need to know. I'm just glad to know about it," Big Jim said.

"I have my sources, which as you know, I cannot divulge," Annie answered mysteriously with a wink. They all groaned. "Oh, all right. The editor asked me what I was looking for and he remembered a story on the Malbon Gang."

"So, Paul was a member of an Irish mob," Deloris said, thinking out loud. "That means that George and Gordon must be mob members too."

"Hmm, wish we knew this when we grilled those birds this morning," Austin said ruefully to Big Jim.

"Hey, we can get them back in the bird cage. That's why we kept them in the cooler, remember?" Big Jim encouraged.

"Right. Let's get them back. Oh, will you girls be okay if we split?"

"Yes, we're fine. Go get them, tiger," Annie replied.

After they finished eating, Annie headed out to search

for more information on the Malbon Gang and Deloris claimed that she was going home.

When Austin and Big Jim were out of sight, however, Deloris returned to the police station and snuck back to her listening perch in the ladies' restroom. When she got there, George was yelling, "Get me out of this cooler!"

"We will, but first we need to ask you a few more questions. What can you tell us about the Malbon Gang?" Austin asked.

"The what?"

"You heard me, pigeon. Talk!"

"Quit riding me, flatfoot. I got nothing to say."

"Oh, so you're dummying up on me, are you?"

"I ain't no stool pigeon. You can't put a finger on me. I didn't do anything."

"Sit up straight. We don't like you rearing back on our chairs. Put the legs down and show some respect."

"Why? I'm comfortable."

Deloris heard a commotion and what sounded like the chair legs hitting the floor hard.

"You didn't have to kick the chair."

"Okay, let's put you back in stir and see what you say tomorrow."

Deloris heard the door open and with his voice trailing off George said, "I've got rights you know."

"Get him outta here," Austin yelled. "Where's Gordon Nelson?"

George was taken away, and Gordon was brought in.

She heard Austin ask Gordon the same questions, but all he said when asked, was, "I'd rather take my chances with the police than be a canary and sing about the Malbon Gang."

After Gordon was taken back to his cell, Deloris heard

Big Jim tell Austin, "We can hold them for twenty-four hours so let's see what they say early tomorrow morning before they are released."

"Sounds good to me. Hey, we still need to question that other guy, Wanda's son. What's his name?" Deloris heard Austin rustle through some papers. "Yeah, Terry Phillips."

"Right," Big Jim replied. "Do we have an address for him?"

"No, but his mother lives at Thelma's, we can ask her."

"Sounds good. We'll head there next."

As Deloris was stepping down from her perch, she heard someone come into the restroom. After they entered the stall next to her, she quickly flushed the stool and stepped out, washed her hands, and quickly exited. Running outside, she found that she was just in time to catch the bus for home.

CHAPTER 25
Thelma's House

When Austin and Big Jim took off for Thelma's boarding house, it was nearing five o'clock. When they pulled up, Deloris was walking down the street from the bus stop. They must have been delayed and she was relieved that she didn't miss anything.

"Hey, what are you guys doing here?" she asked innocently.

"We need to ask Wanda where to find her son," Austin replied.

"Oh okay. Well come on in," Deloris said as she opened the door and stepped back to give them entrance.

"No, after you," Big Jim insisted.

"Thank you. Hey, everyone! Look who I found outside," Deloris called out. Thelma was in the kitchen with Gracie and Annie fixing a meal, Wanda was setting the table, and Leota was keeping the girls occupied in the living room.

Thelma peeked around the kitchen door that Gracie had opened in order to put the rolls on the dining table and called out to Austin and Big Jim. "Do you want to stay for supper? We're having pot roast." Thelma always cooked enough food for an army so there was plenty to go around.

"I wish we could," Austin walked to the kitchen as he replied. "Regrettably, we have more work to do tonight. We've come to talk with Wanda."

At that, Wanda dropped the forks she had in her hands and looked up at them. "Why, why do you want to see me?" She quickly took a seat in one of the chairs.

"Oh no, relax. We just want to ask you if you know where we can find your son," Big Jim said gently.

"Uh, no. No, I don't. He hasn't been around for a few weeks and I don't know where his *girlfriend,* lives." She said this through gritted teeth. "He was kicked out of his apartment a while back and lives with her now."

Deloris and Annie glanced at each other and slyly shook their heads. Seeing this, Austin persisted. "You're sure you don't know where we can find him?"

"No, Officer. I told you that I don't," Wanda said, starting to get a little testy.

"Well, will you let us know if you hear from him or if he comes by?"

Regaining her composure she replied, "I sure will, Officer," and took the card Big Jim was handing her. He watched her for a moment or two and then turned to leave.

"All right ladies. If any of you see Terry Phillips, you let us know, please," Big Jim said as he walked out the door with Austin and Deloris following closely behind.

"What do you think about that lady's response to us?" he said to Austin as they walked down the sidewalk.

"Something is fishy about it," Deloris said. "I know she's seen Terry recently. He was talking to her in the alley three weeks ago, and she usually goes to visit him on the weekend."

"Exactly," Austin agreed. "She knows more than she is saying. I bet she knows where Terry is. Deloris, go back inside and keep an eye on her for us."

"Let's hang around the corner and watch to see if she comes out of the house and leads us to him," Big Jim suggested as they climbed into the car.

"Let's skedaddle."

Big Jim looked at Austin, "What is that?"

"I heard it somewhere," Austin said with a big smile.

"Well stop that. It doesn't fit a crime-fighting gumshoe's character. You've got to be a tough guy."

"Right," Austin looked embarrassed. He turned around and saw Deloris had stealthily climbed into the backseat. "What do you think you're doing?"

"I need to help you find Terry since you don't know what he looks like."

Austin relented and Big Jim started the car and moved it to the next street where he turned it around to face Thelma's house with a good view of both sides.

As they waited, Austin hit Big Jim on the shoulder and said, "Is that tough enough for you?"

"You're kidding right? That was a weak sister kind of punch."

"I didn't want to hurt you." Austin replied.

"Boys!" Deloris interrupted, "Look!"

Big Jim and Austin looked in the direction she was pointing and saw Wanda coming out of the back of the house and going to the garage behind it. She went inside and closed the door behind her.

Big Jim put his hands on the wheel, ready to follow Wanda's car, but the garage doors didn't open. They watched the doors for a short time and before exiting the car, Big Jim turned to Deloris and said, "Stay here!" He and

Austin quietly walked toward the garage and Deloris followed. Outside the building they paused to listen a moment and they heard a man and a woman arguing. He signaled to Austin to open the door. Big Jim pulled his police-issued revolver and had a flashlight at the ready. When Austin swung the door open, there stood Wanda and Terry, with a cross between surprise and horror on their faces.

"You lied to us, Wanda. Why did you do that? We only wanted to talk to your son," Big Jim chastised.

"I, I didn't know he was here. I was just coming out to get something out of my car and found him here," Wanda stuttered.

"Thanks, Mom. You stupid cow!"

"Terry, honey. Be nice," Wanda pleaded.

Terry groaned and shook his head in exasperation.

"Okay, you two are coming down to the station with us," Big Jim stated as he grabbed Terry's arm and pulled him toward the door. As Big Jim turned back to the police car, he saw Deloris, sighed, and shook his head. "I thought I told you to stay in the car. Which of course you didn't do." Deloris shrugged with a wry smile.

Austin took Wanda's arm. "Wait, I need to get my purse," she pleaded.

"Okay, but I'm coming with you," Austin countered.

With Deloris following, Austin took Wanda into the back of the house through the door that led directly to her bedroom. He stood there while she looked for her purse. She was obviously stalling. When Austin bent down to try and help her find it, she hit him over the head with a washboard. It didn't knock him out, but it sure hurt. He reached up and grabbed her arm as she started to hit him again, but Deloris snatched the washboard away. Wanda wrenched and writhed to get out of Austin's grasp, but he held firm as he stood up to face her.

"Okay, ma'am. Looks like you're spending the night in the slammer."

"Lay off of me, you big goon! Let go! I don't trust coppers," Wanda said as she continued to squirm and kick.

Both Deloris and Austin were shocked at Wanda's transformation. She was suddenly showing a different persona than the sweet older lady she usually portrayed at home.

Austin grabbed his handcuffs with his free hand and quickly got her cuffed. With all of the commotion and shouting, the other residents of the house came to her bedroom's inside door and started knocking.

"Wanda, is everything okay?" Thelma asked through the door.

Austin yelled back, "Everything is under control. It's me, Austin."

Deloris opened the door to find Thelma, Annie and Gracie all waiting on the other side.

Austin continued, "Wanda is coming down to the station with us. Don't expect her back tonight. Can you call for a paddy wagon for us? And you might make sure this back door is locked when we leave. We'll have officers come back to search her room tomorrow."

"Of course. Sure thing," Thelma replied in a state of shock.

Austin glared at Wanda as he guided her out the back door and down the steps with Deloris behind him. He met up with Big Jim who had Terry in handcuffs, too. Within minutes the paddy wagon arrived and whisked Wanda and Terry away, leaving Austin, Big Jim, and Deloris standing in the driveway. Thelma, who had been watching from Wanda's back door, came out carrying some meatloaf.

"Hang on. Before you two leave, I packaged this up earlier and wanted to give it to you since you didn't have time to eat. Take this," Thelma said, handing Austin the food. "Deloris can get the dishes back from you tomorrow at the station."

"Thanks," said Austin

"Are you going to interrogate them tonight?" Deloris asked.

"No," Big Jim replied, "We'll talk to them tomorrow morning. A night in jail should soften them up. I'm going home. I'm tired. How about you, Austin?"

"I could use a good night's sleep."

CHAPTER 26

Terry the Terrible

The next day, a windy Tuesday morning, Deloris arranged for Gracie to cover for her at the switchboard, and she went in the back door to the station house. There was only one other officer coming in ahead of her, so no one saw her enter. Looking around, she didn't see Austin or Big Jim, which was good. As she neared the first-floor ladies' restroom, she reached into her purse and pulled out an "Out of Order" sign. This time, she had planned ahead. Looking around, everyone was preoccupied with someone or something, so she quickly taped the sign on the door of the restroom and slipped inside, locking it behind her. Then she pushed the big trash can against the door. Hearing voices coming down the hallway, she took up her perch on the toilet. Before long, she heard the door to the interrogation room being swung open with a bang, and Big Jim said, "Austin, get in here. Now."

Austin entered and said, "What's going on? I thought you went to check on George and Gordon?"

Big Jim slammed the door shut and said, "I did."

"What happened down there?"

"Someone beat up our prisoners, the Nelson brothers."

"What? Who?"

"I don't know, but I intend to get to the bottom of it." Big Jim opened the door and called the guard whom he brought with him from the cells, to come in.

"Which cop did this?" Big Jim asked the guard, sounding utterly furious.

"Did what?"

"Which cop went into the cells of George and Gordon Nelson and beat them up last night?"

"I... I don't know sir. I stepped away to go to the john and when I returned, they were like that."

Sounds like a convenient excuse, Deloris thought.

"If I find out you had anything to do with this, I'll have your badge. Do you understand?"

"Yes, sir."

"If anything else happens to them, I am going to hold you and whomever relieves you personally responsible. Do you understand that?"

"Yes, sir."

"You can go home now, but remember I don't want to see so much as a new bruise on either one of them."

Wow, Deloris thought. She had never heard Big Jim this angry.

She could hear the door open and close so she assumed the guard left the room. There was a moment of silence, and then Big Jim sighed,

"We have to tell the Captain."

"I'll go get him," Austin said and Deloris heard him leave.

A minute later, he returned and she could hear Captain Denton say, "Hi Jim. What's going on?"

Deloris listened as the two detectives explained what

happened. Captain Denton asked if Mrs. Phillips and her son were all right, and Big Jim assured him that they were.

"I'll get to the bottom of this," Denton said. "You two focus on solving the Sullivan murder." Captain Denton left, and she heard Big Jim tell the guard to bring in Terry Phillips.

"Have a seat there."

She heard a chair scrape the floor as it was pulled away from the table.

Big Jim started the questioning, "Okay. Tell me your name for the record."

In a weak voice, Terry responded, "My name is Terrence Phillips."

"Where do you live, Terrence Phillips?"

"You, you can call me Terry, everyone does. I live with my girlfriend in an apartment off of Summit." Deloris thought Terry was obviously trying to ingratiate himself with Big Jim.

"Okay, Terrence," Big Jim didn't respond to Terry's attempt and Deloris smirked. "I understand that you knew Paul Sullivan. How do you know Paul?"

"We went to school together."

"Okay, I need your full accounting of last Friday night."

"Friday night? Let's see. Well, I went to see my mother around 4 p.m. and then Maizie and I went out to eat and then to a party."

"Where did you go eat?" Big Jim asked, starting to quicken the pace of questions.

"Venetian Gardens."

"Did anyone see you there?"

"No."

"Where was the party?"

"It was at this guy's house over on Lawn Street."

"Do you know his name?"

"Nah, some friend of my buddy's."

"Which buddy?"

"Gordon Nelson."

"Was Paul Sullivan at the party?"

"Yeah, but he left a little before 10:00 p.m. when a bunch of cops came and tried to break up the party."

"Ten? I heard that he left earlier."

"No, I'm pretty sure it was 10 p.m. because right after he left, Maizie said it was 10 p.m. and we should leave too."

"Where were you at 10:30 p.m.?"

"I was with my girlfriend. We went to her place."

"Will she vouch for you?

"Yeah, I'm sure she will. I stayed all weekend at her place."

"What's her name again?"

"Maizie."

"Her full name."

"I don't know."

"You don't know the full name of your girlfriend?" Austin interrupted with an incredulous sound in his voice.

"It's something like Smith. Wait, Smythe. S-M-Y-T-H-E. Yeah, that's it. Smythe. Maizie Smythe."

"Did you murder Paul Sullivan?" Big Jim asked, trying to catch Terry off guard.

"No! I swear I didn't kill him. Why would I? He was my best friend and the only person who ever treated me right."

"Didn't he have a part in beating you up?"

"Well yeah, but I deserved it. Paul really only watched. He didn't hit me."

"How's that? You deserved it?"

"I, uh, kind of owed them some money, George and Gordon that is."

"Didn't that make you angry that Paul watched and didn't stop them?"

"Naw, Those mugs rough me up all the time. I was angrier at Gordon."

"Why?"

"I can't say."

"You better come clean in here. It can only help you."

"If I say anything, I'll get killed."

"Oh really? Did Gordon kill Paul?"

"I don't know, but he does lose his temper often. Paul could have said something that ticked him off if he tried to stop him."

"What about George?"

"Naw, Gordon is more likely to kill someone rather than George. George is always trying to calm Gordon down, but I ain't ratting either of them out. I don't know who did it, but it wasn't me!"

Deloris thought Terry was telling the truth. If he wasn't mad at Paul for the beating, it didn't seem likely that he would have killed Paul.

"I want to go back to the money," said Austin.

"What money?"

"The money you owed George and Gordon."

"What about it?"

"Why did you owe them money?"

"I, uh, I lost a bet."

"You lost a bet, huh?"

"Yep," said Terry, sounding more confident.

"Then why did George tell us that it was because you stole some things at the Adcock house robbery you didn't tell the Nelson brothers about? Gordon said you were trying to pawn off things on the side, without giving the brothers their cut."

Deloris was a little surprised at that statement and thought that she didn't remember hearing George or Gordon say that.

"Those lousy, double-crossing greaseballs! They're trying to rat me out, but it's a lie! I didn't take anything from the gang. All the money from that ritzy couple's stuff we divided up evenly, and it was Paul who pawned it, not me! George and Gordon beat me up 'cause I wanted to leave. I was gonna elope with Maizie and leave the gang and they said I couldn't 'cause I knew too much and they needed me for a job next week. We were gonna rob this wealthy widow who'd just taken a bunch of securities home from the bank."

"You were going to rob a widow?"

"No, no, I was the lookout, see? Paul drove the getaway car, I was the lookout, and George and Gordon were the ones who were gonna toss the dame."

"Terrence Phillips," said Big Jim, "I am charging you with robbery, attempted robbery, and probably lots of other things once we get George and Gordon to testify against you.

After a moment of stunned silence, Terry asked, "George and Gordon didn't say nothing to you coppers?"

"Pal," Big Jim replied, "not a word."

"Oh man. My goose is cooked."

CHAPTER 27

Juanita Connors

Deloris climbed down from her perch on the toilet and stretched her back while Terry was taken away and booked. She really needed to figure out how to listen without standing on a toilet seat. She wondered if she could sneak a ladder of some kind into the restroom, mark the stall out of order, and then set it up there. Why didn't she think of that sooner? At least with the sign up, no one had come into the restroom this time. She was just lucky before, though it probably helped that all of the police officers were men and only a few women were on the first floor. The switchboard ladies used the restroom on the second floor. Then she heard voices again, and the door to the interrogation room opened. She climbed back up to listen.

"Why do you have me here?" Wanda asked in a perfectly polite voice.

"Well, for starters, you assaulted an officer, you knowingly withheld information, *and* you were harboring a fugitive from the law," Austin began.

"I told you that I didn't know Terry was in the garage."

"I don't believe you."

With that, it was like Wanda flipped on a switch again and sounded like another person, Deloris thought. She went from a sweet, motherly type to a vicious bear.

"I want to see my boy!" she said forcefully.

"You can see him if you answer our questions truthfully. What do you know about Paul Sullivan's murder? Did your son do it?"

"No, no. I don't know anything about Paul Sullivan's murder and *no,* my son didn't murder him. Can I go now?"

"No, Mrs. Phillips," Big Jim took over the questioning. "You can't go just yet. What were you doing at the party at Walter McKinley's house Friday night?"

Wanda's face changed to a look of surprise. "I, I wasn't at any party."

"We have a witness who says you were there."

"Well, I was only there for a minute. I needed to see my son. I needed him to listen to reason, and to get away from those people at the party and especially from that woman he was with before he got into any trouble."

"What trouble did you think he would get into?"

"I don't know. I just know that George and Gordon are always in trouble and that Maizie is no better. She's a bad influence on my Terry and mean to him. She doesn't treat him right!"

There came a knock at the door. "Yes?" Big Jim asked.

"I have some new information for you, sir," said the voice at the door.

"Let's take this out in the hall. I'll be right back," Big Jim said and he stepped out of the room. As luck would have it, he stood right under the open transom window above the door to the ladies' restroom, so Deloris could hear this conversation clearly as well.

"I've been checking the fingerprints for your new detainees, and I found both in the system." Deloris tried to place the new voice, and eventually realized it was Sergeant Cox.

"Both, really? Do tell us more, but keep your voice down because these walls are paper thin," Austin said, not sounding surprised. So, Austin had obviously stepped outside too.

Deloris carefully stepped down from the toilet and crept closer to the door.

"Terrence Phillips has a rap sheet this thick with petty theft and robbery," the sergeant continued. "But Mrs. Phillips comes up as a Juanita Connors and again as Juanita McKinley. As Juanita Connors she was suspected of being in a gang, the Malbon Gang, they called themselves. They did several bank robberies with one murder—a security guard at a bank. Her boyfriend was caught, found guilty of the murder, and sent to prison where he was executed."

"Very interesting," Big Jim said.

"Why wasn't Juanita arrested?" Austin asked.

"I'm not sure. The evidence was only circumstantial, maybe they didn't think they had enough on her to make it stick. Maybe she knew somebody on the force."

Another dirty cop? Deloris thought. That would explain why Wanda hadn't been arrested. Or maybe, even why George and Gordon were beaten up last night.

Sergeant Cox continued, "She was then married to a guy named Zachariah McKinley, a small-time penny ante thief. At least, he was small time until he hooked up with her and joined the Malbon Gang. Juanita McKinley is wanted for a series of bank robberies, and assault with a deadly weapon. Zachariah McKinley was arrested for a botched armed robbery and sent to prison, where he still resides. Under the name Juanita McKinley, there are some charges that will stick, but she escaped when Zachariah McKinley was caught, and then just disappeared. With no signs of the gang for decades, it was assumed that she died or left the area."

"So, Wanda Phillips is really Juanita McKinley or Juanita Connors." Austin sounded stunned.

"Yep," said Sergeant Cox.

"Okay, thank you Sergeant. Let us know if you find anything else."

"Yes, sir. I'll keep digging through the old Malbon Gang files. I knew you were interrogating Wanda and I thought you should know this so I ran up here as quick as I could."

"Yes, that is good work. Thank you, Sergeant."

Deloris heard the door to the interrogation room open and close. She ran back to the stall and stepped up. Her foot slipped and she almost stepped into the water, but she quickly grabbed the side of the stall to steady herself.

"Wanda Phillips," Big Jim said, "Or should I say Juanita?"

"Who? My name isn't Juanita, it's Wanda. You have me confused with somebody else."

"Come now, Juanita. Has it been too many years calling yourself Wanda that you forgot your real name? Where did you get the name Phillips?"

"It was my husband's name, you doofus."

"And what was your husband's name?"

"Albert, Albert Phillips. You can look him up. He is real, or was until he passed away several years ago."

"I will. How did he die?

"He got shot in a train robbery."

"Was he robbing the train?"

"No! He was working for the railroad."

"When was this?"

"Ten years ago."

"Which train was it?"

"It was the Rock Island Railroad."

"I see. So, you married this Albert Phillips and got a whole new name, then you laid low for several years and just recently resurrected your theft ring. Right?"

Wanda didn't offer an answer to that question.

Austin asked, "What do you know about the Malbon Gang?"

"Nothing, I don't know what you're talking about, this Mal-something."

"Malbon, an ancient Celtic symbol used by the Malbon Gang thirty years ago. How old would you have been thirty years ago, Mrs. Phillips?"

"You have my file there. You figure it out."

"You would have been in your twenties, is that correct?"

"I don't know."

"Come now, Mrs. Phillips. I bet you know something about it. Did you know anyone in the gang? Were you a member?"

"No! I don't know what you are talking about."

The more she protested, the more Austin persisted.

"Look, we've got you dead to rights in a series of bank robberies, train robberies and murder. Your fingerprints matched up and you are going away for a long time, Juanita or Wanda or whatever you want to call yourself. So, what happened? You got George, Gordon, Paul, and Terry to start robbing the affluent neighborhoods for you? It was easy for you to know who to target, working as a bank teller, wasn't it?"

"No, it wasn't like that at all," Wanda said.

"How was it, then?" Austin asked.

"Walt McKinley saw me at Thelma's house. He was my stepson once-upon-a- time, when I was married to his father, Zach, before Terry was born. He told George, who told Gordon. Gordon threatened to expose me to the cops if I didn't help them with who to target for robberies. George came up with the idea to resurrect the gang and its symbol. They recruited my Terry and Paul to help them. Paul fenced the stolen goods and gave them the money to distribute."

"Why did they beat Terry up?"

"He wanted to quit the gang and I did, too. I told them that I wasn't giving them any more information because I was afraid of getting caught. That's when they beat my Terry up—threatening to do worse—if I quit the gang."

"Where were you Friday night at 10 p.m.?

"I was at home in bed. I went directly home when I left the party. You saw me, remember, or is your memory gone?" Wanda said indignantly.

"So, who killed Paul?"

"I don't know officer, but I swear it wasn't Terry." Wanda said agitatedly.

"That may be, but he confessed to being part of a robbery gang earlier this morning, and he's under arrest," Austin said. "Which is too bad, because we've got a dirty cop here. Heaven help Terry if that cop who roughed up Gordon and George gets to him, too."

"What? Gordon and George were attacked? By who?"

"We don't know, but we are working to find that out."

"It happened here in jail?"

"Yep," Austin replied flippantly.

"Wait, if I tell you something can Terry be released? Or get a lesser sentence?"

"Well, that depends upon what you're going to tell us," Big Jim said.

"Can you at least protect my Terry from the guy who got to Gordon and George? I think I know who it was."

"If you can tell us who, we can make sure that person doesn't get anywhere near you or Terry."

There was a long pause, and when Wanda spoke again, she sounded resigned to her fate. "Okay, well there is a cop here who has been with the police force for several years. He turns a blind eye to the heists only if he gets a cut. He sends word by using the Malbon symbol, telling us where to meet him to give him his cut, or if he needs any information from us."

"Do you know his name?"

"Detective Timothy O'Malley," Wanda replied softly. "He claimed we shorted him. I am certain that he beat up George and Gordon because he was afraid that they would rat him out. He probably killed Paul because of it, too."

"I see," Austin said.

"What about Maizie?" Austin asked. "I thought they jumped Terry because he was going to elope with Maizie and leave the gang."

"Mazie?" Wanda laughed. "Maizie is still married to the last sap, and Terry knows it." After a pause, she continued,

"He was just trying to protect me. He's a good son, most of the time."

Big Jim called for the guard to have Wanda taken back to her cell.

"You are going to protect my Terry, right?"

"We will do everything we can to make sure he and you will be safe," Austin replied.

"I hope so," she said as she left with the guard.

CHAPTER 28

Crooked

Once Wanda had been escorted away, Deloris heard Austin ask, "Of all people, why did it have to be O'Malley? Do you think he could have killed Paul Sullivan?"

"We need to take it to Captain Denton and see what he says. But if O'Malley killed Paul, we better make sure we have absolute proof," Big Jim replied.

"Yeah, I guess so. What do you think the captain will do?"

"He'll probably take it to the chief, and who knows what they'll do to O'Malley. I'll go get the captain and bring him in here, so it looks like we're briefing him on the case. I don't want to raise any suspicions."

A few minutes later, Deloris heard the door opening again as Big Jim and Captain Denton entered the room.

"What did you find out?" Denton asked enthusiastically.

"Well, Terry confessed that he took part in the robberies, but he didn't kill Paul. With his statement, we can charge George and Gordon with robbery as well," Austin said.

"And we got Wanda Phillips. Her real name is Juanita Connor and then Juanita McKinley. She told us about the Malbon Gang and the theft ring, but we still don't have a lead on who killed Paul."

"Juanita Connor sounds familiar," the captain reflected.

"Yes, she flew the coop when her boyfriend was convicted and executed for murder."

"Oh yes, I remember that case now."

"I think that we need to get George and Gordon back in here and talk with them again," Austin added. "My money's on Gordon for the murder."

"But there's something else, sir," Big Jim said hesitantly. "Wanda told us that Detective O'Malley was getting a take from the heists with the promise to look the other way. He was using the Malbon symbol to set up meetings with the gang to get his cut or if he needed to talk with them. Plus, she made it clear that he and a few other policemen went to the party where Paul Sullivan was last seen before being killed. One of our suspects said that Paul left as soon as the police showed up and O'Malley could have killed him for shorting him of his take from the last robbery."

"Are you kidding me?" Denton almost screamed and then became silent.

"I wish I was," Big Jim said.

"Do you think he killed Paul?"

At that, both detectives remained silent. After a few seconds, Denton asked, "And you believe this Wanda or Juanita?"

"How else would she know his name?" Austin pointed out.

Denton opened the door and called out, "Hey, bring

Sergeant Cox in here." He continued, "The only proof we have is the beating of George and Gordon Nelson, but I can approach him with that and see what I find out."

After a minute, the door opened again. "You wanted me, sir?" Sergeant Cox asked.

"Yes. You covered the evening shift at the front desk yesterday, right?" Denton said.

"Yeah, the night desk sergeant had a bad cold, I told him to go home and I'd stay late."

"Did you see any officers here who weren't on the schedule?"

"Nope, it was pretty quiet last night. No—wait. O'Malley was here, I didn't see him come in, but I swear I caught a glimpse of him going downstairs to the cells. Figured he was talking to his buddy, the night guard. The two of them are good pals."

There was a pause, and then Sergeant Cox said, "Is something wrong? Be on the level, Captain. What's this all about?"

"I promise I'll tell you, but I can't right now," Denton said. "I'm going to need you for a formal statement later and I'll call you into my office at that time. Oh, and thanks, Sergeant."

After the sergeant left the room, Captain Denton said, "Right. After I detain O'Malley, I'll have a chat with George and Gordon, see if they'll 'fess up and tell us if it was O'Malley who knocked them about last night."

"Yes, sir," Austin said.

"I want as many witnesses as possible. O'Malley had time, opportunity, and a motive. You understand that allegations such as these are very serious and if we don't have all of the information, we could all lose our badges—you, me and Big Jim."

"I understand, but he needs to be stopped. I don't like crooked cops, especially if they're murderers," Big Jim replied.

"I don't either, but we don't know if he murdered anyone. I need to find that out first," Denton said. "We can arrest him on suspicion of assault, based on what Wanda told us and Sergeant Cox corroborated. That'll give us time to investigate and see if he's the one who killed Paul Sullivan. I'm going to tell the chief right now and then have a chat with O'Malley."

As Denton left the interrogation room, Deloris heard him call out, "Detective O'Malley, in my office. Now!"

Deloris then heard Big Jim and Austin leave the room, and she figured they weren't coming back any time soon. So, she put everything back in place and snuck out of the restroom, grabbing the sign and putting it back in her purse. Just as she snapped her purse closed, an officer came down the hallway and she smiled at him as they passed. He smiled back in an interested way and she hurried down the hall to the detectives' room, not daring to look back. She found Austin and Big Jim standing outside Captain Denton's door.

"Hey what's up, buttercup?" she said when she got close to their desks. "You want to go to lunch?"

"Shhhh," Austin replied with his finger to his lips.

She could hear Captain Denton and O'Malley yelling at each other through the transom over the door. Big Jim and Austin were obviously listening to the conversation inside, so she joined them.

They could see the shadow of O'Malley at the door with his hand on the doorknob, as he said, "You've got a lot of nerve. I'll have your badge for this and anyone else who is involved!"

Austin and Big Jim jumped back to their desks and Deloris ran to sit down in the chair next to Austin's desk. Both men started shuffling papers on their desk, trying to look busy.

O'Malley threw the door open and stopped to glare at the threesome, then he stopped in front of Deloris with a look of murder in his eyes. After a moment, he stormed out of the detectives' room.

"Yeah, we were just going to eat," Austin said after a minute of silence.

"Mind if I join you?" Deloris requested.

"Not at all," Big Jim replied.

Captain Denton came out of his office, shaking his head. He was surprised and embarrassed to see Deloris there, knowing she had obviously overhead the heated conversation.

"I'm sorry you had to hear that."

"That's okay, Captain. I've heard worse," Deloris said sympathetically.

As they walked to lunch at a diner few blocks away on Manchester Street, the wind was blowing so hard that Deloris had to hold her skirt down and hang on to her hat. She wished that she'd worn a different hat, one that tied under her chin would have been easier to hold on to. After they were seated with their lunches, Deloris guilelessly asked them how solving the robbery case was coming along since they'd arrested Wanda and Terry.

"We've cracked the Malbon Gang robbery case," Big Jim said with a smile.

"That's wonderful," she congratulated them.

"You suspected George, Gordon, Terry, and Paul were all involved, and you were right," Austin said. "But we still don't know who killed Paul Sullivan."

"It wasn't Gordon? Or George?"

"Doesn't look like it," Big Jim said.

"Maybe I can help. It never hurts to have a fresh mind look at the puzzle pieces, you know. Can you go over every suspect and their alibis?" Deloris encouraged.

"Well, Terry is innocent because he spent all Friday evening with his girlfriend," Big Jim started, "at a party with lots of witnesses."

"Yeah, and Wanda was at home in bed. We were at Thelma's for Annie's party, and we saw her go to bed at 9 p.m." Austin said.

"George was sick in bed with the chicken pox and Gordon was at the party at Walter McKinley's place with Terry and Maizie and he stayed until well after midnight."

"Whose party?" Deloris asked with a surprised look upon her face, like she didn't already know the answer.

"Walter McKinley," Austin answered.

"Oh, he was Thelma's second husband. What in the world was he doing throwing a party?"

"They said it was his get-out-of-jail party," Big Jim replied.

"Oh, that makes sense, but I didn't know he knew any of them."

"Well, his father was married to Wanda, I mean Juanita Phillips," Austin said.

"Who?"

"Oh yeah, Wanda's real name is Juanita, and she was married to Zachariah McKinley before she married Albert Phillips. She was a member of the original Malbon Gang but has been lying low for several years. She thought that she had all of that buried, but Walter McKinley saw her at Thelma's and told Gordon."

"That is crazy that both Wanda, I mean Juanita, and

Thelma were married to a father and son," Deloris shook her head.

"Not so crazy. Wanda probably wasn't aware that he had been married to Thelma and was shocked to see him at her boarding house one day. When McKinley saw Wanda, she tried to duck out to her room, but he recognized her immediately even though she changed the color and style of her hair. When Gordon heard about it, he confronted Wanda and threatened to reveal her true identity unless she helped him and George in a series of robberies. He wanted to resurrect the Malbon Gang."

"Hey what was all that about with the Captain?" she asked. She wanted to get Austin to tell her, so that she didn't mess up and say something that she wasn't supposed to know from her listening room.

"Oh, it was police business, Deloris. You don't need to know everything that goes on in the station."

Annoyed at this, she exclaimed, "Well, that's just peachy. See if I give you any more clues!"

A few minutes later, a familiar voice said, "I thought that I'd find you three here," and Captain Denton came up behind the group at the diner.

"Oh, hello, Captain Denton, sir," Austin said half starting to stand.

He waved him to sit down. "Mind if I join you?"

"Please, have a seat," they all said, almost in unison.

As he sat, the waitress came to the table and he ordered a sandwich and a cup of coffee. "I thought that I'd give you an update on the other case, but we can talk when we get back to the office." He glanced at Deloris when he said this.

"The other?" Deloris asked.

"Oh, uh, just something the boys here told me to ask about," he said.

Deloris wasn't surprised that Captain Denton didn't readily tell her about Detective O'Malley, since that was an internal matter and they didn't want anyone to know that they had a crooked cop—possibly a murderer—on the force. It would be a black eye on the whole police force if one was bad.

"You mean it's something about Detective O'Malley?" Deloris asked.

The three men turned their eyes toward Deloris in disbelief that she'd figured it out that quickly. "I was at Austin's desk, I couldn't help but overhear," she said.

"Yes, well, first, since Deloris already knows our darkest secret, I presume she knows all the rest," said Captain Denton. He gave her a knowing nod and continued, "Detective O'Malley is turning the robbery case completely over to you two because he decided to retire. He gave his two weeks' notice this morning. Second, George and Gordon Nelson are cooperating fully and singing like canaries. It was O'Malley and a few other policemen who raided the party."

By the look on Austin and Big Jim's faces, Deloris could tell this was good news.

"They confessed to pulling off at least twenty robberies and will testify against the person who was extorting them for a piece of the take."

"That's excellent, sir!" she said.

"Oh, and by the way," Captain Denton, continued, looking at both Big Jim and Austin, "the Chief was very impressed with your investigation. If you can solve the murder case, you both may get big promotions out of this." Looking at Big Jim he continued, "You may make Lead Detective." Turning to Austin, he said, "I know that you haven't been a junior detective for very long, but if you can crack this case, the Chief would even consider promoting you to full detective and circumventing the regular time period required. Would you recommend and agree with that promotion, Detective Anderson?"

"Absolutely!" Big Jim responded enthusiastically.

"We're on it," Austin replied eagerly.

After lunch, Captain Denton and Big Jim left together discussing the developments. Austin started to leave with them, but Deloris asked him to stay a little while longer and he agreed.

"So, fill me in on the details," Deloris urged.

"Okay, okay. We found a dirty cop who we think was involved with the gang."

"Really? Was it O'Malley?"

"Why do you think it was him?"

"I figured he was stupid enough to get involved in some shady dealings."

"Well, you are correct."

"I knew it!" Deloris said triumphantly.

"Well, you heard the explosion in the captain's office. As it turned out, O'Malley was helping the gang by turning a blind eye to the robberies for a cut. We did a little research and believe that he probably helped the original gang, too, as a young cop. When he arrested George and Gordon sometime in the past six months, he must have learned that they resurrected the Malbon Gang, so he cut himself in and came up with using the symbol again."

"That is unbelievable. I mean, I can see O'Malley as a dirty detective, but dear sweet Wanda, I mean Juanita, a gang member?"

"No, Juanita was a gang leader first, then a gang member," Austin corrected.

"Who would have thought? And her in Thelma's house. That is disturbing," Deloris said, shaking her head. "I'll need to tell Thelma all of this gently. She will be very upset."

"You can't tell her about any of this until it goes to trial, and you *especially* can't mention Detective O'Malley."

"I won't tell her about O'Malley, but she needs to know about Wanda and the robberies. I still can't believe it. She was so nice. Do you think O'Malley killed Paul?"""

"We don't know if he did or not. You just never know about people and the secrets they keep."

Where had Deloris heard that recently? Oh yes, it was when she was talking to Wanda—Juanita. How ironic.

CHAPTER 29

The Alibi

Deloris headed home after the lunch and anxiously waited for Thelma to get home after her shift at Leed's Lunch Counter. She couldn't wait to tell her about Wanda—or Juanita—or whatever her name really was.

While she waited, she thought that it wouldn't hurt if she went into Wanda's room and looked around even though the police had searched it pretty thoroughly that morning. Everything was in total disarray, total chaos—unlike how Wanda kept her room—neat as a pin. Clothes were spilling out of the dresser and clothes that had been hanging in the wardrobe were laying on the bed that had its mattress askew. Deloris looked under the bed and under the stove, but found nothing.

Deloris heard the front door open almost with a bang from the wind pushing it. She left Wanda's room and ran into the kitchen. When Thelma came into the kitchen with the groceries, she was bundled up in a jacket and a head-scarf. Deloris knew that Thelma wouldn't like for her to be snooping around in Wanda's room even if Wanda was in jail.

Deloris sat Thelma down and told her all about Wanda and how she had been the leader of a theft ring thirty years ago and was a part of a gang now.

Thelma listened calmly and said that she remembered hearing about the thefts from an older lady who lived on the other side of the street when she first moved in. Then a thought crossed her mind and a look of concern appeared on her face.

"To think that she was in my house where my family was." Then she asked, "Did you say that she was married to Walter?"

"No, to his father, Zachariah."

"He told me that his father was dead." Thelma became more visibly angry as it all started to sink in. "Was Wanda, or whatever her name is, was she a part of the gang who beat up Marguerite?"

"Yes, I suppose that is true."

"She is out of here! I am throwing her stuff out of the house, and I don't ever want to see her again."

Understanding Thelma's anger, Deloris promised to help Thelma pack up Wanda's things. She then told Thelma that Paul's murderer was still on the loose and that the police hadn't found the murder weapon yet, either. They had ruled out George due to his being sick in bed with the chicken pox. Terry and Gordon were ruled out because they were at a party during the time Paul was murdered. Wanda was ruled out because she was there, in the boarding house in bed, at 9 p.m.

Thelma said thoughtfully, "But Wanda wasn't home *all* evening. She went to her room at 9 p.m. but I noticed her slip out of the back door about 9:30, so I kept watching her.

She headed to the garage, started up her car, and left. I'd gone to bed by then, but I wasn't asleep yet. You were all still partying in the other rooms so you didn't hear her leave. She didn't return until midnight or a little after when the sound of her car and the garage door woke me up. I have a perfect view of the garage and the side door to her room from my bedroom. No, I'm certain that she didn't return home until after midnight."

Deloris blinked in surprise. "We need to tell Austin this information."

"Why don't you ring him up?" Thelma suggested as she went to the coat closet in the hall to hang up her headscarf and jacket.

Seeing Thelma hang up her jacket gave Deloris an idea. The officers had searched Wanda's room, but not her winter coat. Deloris went to the closet and found Wanda's coat hanging at the end of the clothes rod. She pulled it out. It felt heavier than it should have. She ran her hands down the coat and felt something inside the left pocket. She laid it across the sofa and felt the left pocket from the outside. She was certain that she felt the outline of a gun in that pocket. She didn't pull it out in order to preserve fingerprints, but she ran to the phone and called Austin.

Thelma watched all of this in shock, and when Leota came in from the park with the girls, Thelma quickly escorted the group upstairs with the excuse that they needed to have a bath after running around playing in the dirt. She gave Deloris a long, worried look as she went up the stairs.

When Austin arrived, Deloris showed him the coat. He took out his handkerchief and pulled a gun out of the coat pocket. He smelled the barrel and told her that it had been fired recently. Deloris got a paper bag from the kitchen for him to put the gun in.

"Do you think that that's the murder weapon?" Deloris queried.

"I need to have ballistics run tests on it, but it certainly could be," Austin answered.

"Have a seat at the table for a moment and I'll tell you what Thelma said." Deloris pulled out a chair.

"Okay."

"Wanda left the house about 9:30 while we were all still in here partying. Can you believe it?"

"Of course I can. We provided her the perfect alibi."

"I need to get this gun down to the station to have ballistics confirm if it is the murder weapon or not," Austin said, getting up to retrieve his hat and walking to the door. "I'll let you know what I find out. See you tomorrow."

"Thank you," Deloris said. She gave Austin a ten-minute head start, and then called a taxi to take her back to the police station. Thank goodness she still had some of that huge tip that Mr. O'Brien allowed her to keep from the money the soda fountain scammers left behind, Deloris thought. Racing around in taxis wasn't cheap, but she could afford it for now.

When Deloris got to the station she waved at Sergeant Cox and told him she'd forgotten something upstairs in the switchboard office. Then she stole back into the first-floor ladies' restroom just in time to hear Wanda say, "What am I doing back here? I told you everything I know. Is my boy okay?"

"Your son is fine," Big Jim reassured her. "I just have a few more questions for you. We found your gun, Wanda."

"Gun? I don't have a gun."

Big Jim paused, "Then why was it in your coat pocket?"

"I don't know how a gun got there. Someone must have put it there. What coat pocket?"

The door opened and Austin entered, saying, "Hello, Wanda."

"What do you want?"

"The gun we found in your coat pocket is a Colt 1908 Vest Pocket .25 ACP and a match for the bullet taken out of Paul Sullivan's back."

"So?"

"So, we found your fingerprints all over it and no one else's. Plus, it matches a few other crimes from years past. Twenty years ago, a bank security guard was shot and killed with this gun and your boyfriend was executed for the murder, but the gun was never found. Let's not forget that ten years ago, your husband, Albert Phillips, was shot and killed in a botched train robbery. This gun matches that bullet."

"Oh, really?" Wanda answered nonchalantly.

"Did you kill these men?"

"I tell you it isn't my gun."

"No? Was it your boyfriend's gun that we never found for his trial?"

Wanda was silent.

"Looks like you are going away for a long time, Wanda. Why did you kill Albert?"

Resigned to her fate, Wanda confessed.

"Albert used to beat me and Terry. I saw the opportunity to get rid of him during the robbery and I took it, but look I didn't intend to kill Paul. That was a mistake, I wanted to kill Gordon because Terry and I wanted to leave the gang, and he wouldn't let us. Then he beat my boy pretty badly and threatened to do even worse if I quit helping them. I just wanted him to leave us alone," Wanda pleaded with the detectives. "Don't you see?"

"How did you make a mistake, Juanita? Paul doesn't look anything like Gordon."

Wanda sighed, "Paul always wore a light-colored beige jacket. I never saw him wear a dark-colored jacket and I guess he and Gordon both had black jackets hanging on the coat stand."

"Paul's jacket was dark blue," Austin interrupted.

"See? It was an honest mistake," she insisted. "I must have put the note in Paul's jacket pocket instead of Gordon's by accident at the party. I told him to go behind the soda fountain and wait for me there. Of course, he thought it was O'Malley meeting him. I tried to disguise my handwriting to look like one of O'Malley's notes."

"Go on," Big Jim pushed for Wanda to continue.

"All right. Then it was dark behind the building and I couldn't tell who it was standing there with his back to me. I just saw the dark jacket and fired my gun."

"But why did you have him go to the soda fountain?"

"I knew the park would be deserted and no one would find him until morning, or so I thought. I didn't mean to kill Paul, honest. He was always so good to my Terry." With that, Wanda broke down crying. "I've made a mess of everything."

"Yes, you have." Austin opened the door and told the officer who was standing guard to take Wanda to booking.

CHAPTER 30

The Wrap-up

Wanda was convicted for the murders of both Albert Phillips and Paul Sullivan and as accessory to murder of the bank security guard who was killed when she was Juanita Conner. She was also found guilty of being an accomplice to the robberies undertaken by George, Gordon, Terry, and Paul.

Detective Timothy O'Malley was not prosecuted since he agreed to retire and because he was friends with too many of the other not-so-innocent officers who looked the other way. Captain Denton, however, pushing his superiors as hard as he could, did manage to quietly get O'Malley's pension decreased to that of a junior officer. The night guard who'd let O'Malley into the Nelson brothers' cells the night they were beaten was fired.

George "Brown" and Gordon "Babyface" Nelson were convicted for twenty robberies and the assault and battery of Marguerite and Tommy Adcock.

Terrence "Terry the Terror" Phillips was convicted as an accessory to the robberies, receiving three years in jail as the driver of the getaway vehicle. But the biggest punishment for him was losing his mother, his biggest supporter. How was he going to survive without her when he got out of jail? He was beside himself and played the "poor me" tune to anyone who would listen, but few did. Maizie moved on almost immediately and found a new boyfriend who had lots of money.

A couple months later, Annie brought a newspaper article home to share with Thelma and Deloris. The headline read, "Man, twice convicted, claims he was just showing the bartender his gun." The article went on to say that four policemen were at a 'resort' to conduct a tour and do a possible raid as they looked for a hidden speakeasy selling illegal booze. Two officers were at the front door and two came from the back. One officer went through the kitchen and saw a man tapping on a door behind the bar that led to the hidden speakeasy. When the bartender opened the door, Walter McKinley stuck a gun in his face and said, "Stick 'em up." The officer crept up behind Walter and looked over his shoulder to confirm that he was indeed holding a gun. Then he put his own gun in Walter's ribs and said, "What do you think you're doing? Drop the gun." The door quickly closed, but another officer kicked it in, gaining access to the speakeasy. Walter was arrested along with the folks in the speakeasy.

He whined, "Honest officer, I was just showing the bartender my new gun. I wasn't robbing him. It was just a joke."

Some joke. He wasn't even smart enough to be a successful criminal.

Epilogue

HAPPY ENDING

Deloris, Annie, and Austin went to Mrs. Sullivan's to tell her that the police had Paul's murderer in custody and to collect Thelma's dishes. Mrs. Sullivan had to sit down when they told her about Wanda. "She was Terry's mother, right?"

"Yes," Annie replied.

"I just can't believe that. She and I used to talk about our boys and they were such good friends."

"Hold on to your hat, there's more," Deloris told her, explaining about Wanda's leadership of the Malbon Gang.

When Deloris finished the story, Mrs. Sullivan was stunned.

"Are you okay, Mama?" Mary Margaret asked, concerned at the look on her mother's face.

"Yes, child. I'm all right. I'm just in shock."

"Mrs. Sullivan, I do have some good news for you," Austin added. "Because Wanda is going to be in jail for the rest of her life, she asked that we give you her car saying that perhaps you could sell it. She also wanted you to know how very sorry she is for accidentally killing Paul. She never wanted to hurt him."

Before Mrs. Sullivan could respond, there came a knock at the door and Mary Margaret went to answer it.

"Mama, there's a man here who says that he needs to talk with you," Mary Margaret called from the front door.

"If you'll excuse me." Mrs. Sullivan rose from her chair and walked to the door. She returned with the man at the door, whom Deloris immediately recognized from the soda fountain.

"This man says that he is with a life insurance company. Apparently, Paul took out an insurance policy a few weeks before he was killed."

"Yes, Mrs. Sullivan. You stand to receive a substantial amount of money." The man opened his briefcase and handed her a check. Tentatively taking it, Mrs. Sullivan began to tear up.

"Mama, what is wrong?"

"Nothing, my dear. Your brother is still taking care of us, we're going to be all right."

"Oh, Mama." Crying, Mary Margaret hugged her mother and the two younger children squeezed into the hug to participate.

Austin got up and said, "I think we should go and leave this family to their good news." Deloris and Annie agreed and the three slipped out of the house.

Marguerite was able to recover all her stolen goods except for one piece of jewelry—a brooch that belonged to her mother-in-law. It was a family heirloom, but it was an ugly, ornate Victorian piece that Marguerite had never liked.

Though she was far too well-bred to ever admit it, she was not at all upset that she'd never have to wear it for her mother-in-law again. She and Harry had a healthy baby girl they named Deloris.

Mr. O'Brien was saddened by his cousin's death and feared that it would harm the reputation of Poppy's Paradise Park. However, Annie's reporting made it clear that the murder had nothing to do with Poppy's, and business remained steady. Paul's death left the soda fountain short-handed, but instead of hiring someone else for the rest of the summer, Mr. O'Brien transferred Trudie from the concession stand to help Deloris out on the weekends.

Since Big Jim and Austin not only successfully cracked a robbery ring and solved the murder of Paul Sullivan, but also solved the older cases of the Malbon Gang and the murder of Albert Phillips, Captain Denton recommended to the chief a promotion for Big Jim to Lead Detective and Austin to full detective. Austin hoped now that he was no longer a junior detective, he'd be able to think of something brilliant and profound to say to Carolyn Bechtel.

Austin and Big Jim's promotion ceremony was in July, and Thelma and all her boarders attended, as did Austin's parents and Big Jim's girlfriend. Deloris arranged for Harry, Marguerite, and Tommy Adcock to attend the ceremony as well, and she also talked Austin into giving Tommy a VIP tour of the police station afterward. At the end of the tour, Big Jim and Austin gave Tommy a junior detective badge and a police hat. Tommy put on the police hat with a huge grin and said, "I'm Detective Adcock, and criminals always get caught!"

Captain Denton overheard this remark as he was exiting his office, and with a twinkle in his blue eyes he replied, "You're absolutely right, young man!"

❧

Thelma decided to make a fresh start by cutting her hair and trying a new look. She asked Deloris to find a new boarder for her, since Deloris had done so well in finding Gracie and Thelma had not done so well in finding Wanda.

❧

Annie published her second article, a front page spread in the Sunday morning paper about Wanda, the Nelsons, and the Malbon Gang. She and Deloris bought twenty copies, one of which they clipped out, framed, and hung on the wall in Thelma's kitchen. In the next Thursday's paper, Annie did a follow-up piece about the history of the Malbon Gang and the Celtic symbol. Because of her work on the articles, the editor promoted her to a full-time reporter, but the only opening was on the society pages. Soon, though, Annie promised herself, she'd be back to reporting on crime.

❧

Deloris continued her work at the switchboard and the soda fountain. Leon, finally back in town, took her out on a few dates, fed her all manner of ice cream concoctions, and became a frequent caller at the boarding house. Thelma laughingly complained that she could only understand every third word he said. Though Deloris wouldn't admit it to Thelma, Leon's Chicago accent, coupled with the current slang and topped with soda fountain lingo, made him a bit hard for even her to understand at times.

Deloris thoroughly enjoyed her time shadowing Austin and snooping around. The fact that she found the murder weapon after the police searched for it gave her confidence that she could be a good detective, too. Austin and Big Jim gave her credit for helping them with the case and thanked her. She was a little sad when she thought that life in Kansas City might be quieter now that she had solved the mysteries of Marguerite's robbers and Paul's murderer. Little did she know that she'd be making an unexpected visit back to Jameson in August, and her detecting skills would once more be called into use.

About the Author(s)

Through conversation and stories, two friends who like old movies, mysteries and history started talking about writing a book that featured these elements. One friend has two books published about her mother, Doris Markham. Doris, who lived in Kansas City in the 1930s, experienced some of the stories told in this book. The other friend thought that a detective inspired by Doris Markham would be a great place to begin this writing adventure. As time progressed, the friends developed the Miss Markham Mystery Series. The main character—much like her real-life inspiration—is spunky, hard-headed and fearless. This is the first book of the series; many more of The Miss Markham Mysteries are in the works. The name Juliet E. Sidonie is a combination of the two authors' grandmother's and great-grandmother's names. For more historical content and additional information, visit their website.

MissMarkhamMysteries.com

Definitions

SODA FOUNTAIN TREATS

The Big List of Old-Fashioned Soda Fountain Drink Recipes
https://www.prairiemoon.biz/bigliofoldfa.html

Soda Jerk Slang
https://www.atlasobscura.com/articles/soda-jerk-slang

Acid Phosphate: used to add acidity to drinks. It is a weak
acid made from phosphate.

Black and White: 2 Tbsp. chocolate syrup, 2 scoops vanilla
ice cream, and seltzer.

Canary Island Special: vanilla syrup, seltzer, chocolate ice
cream

Catawba Flip: 1 scoop vanilla ice cream, 1 large egg, 2 oz.
grape juice, shaved ice, seltzer.

Cherry Phosphate: cherry soda made from cherry syrup, phosphate acid and soda water.

Egg Creams: 2 Tbsp. chocolate syrup, 5 oz. milk, 3 oz. seltzer water. (Ironically egg creams don't have any eggs in them.)

Missouri River Ale: Water -- a term made up by the author based upon Hudson River Ale.

Traffic Light Sundae: Three scoops of vanilla ice cream with a red, green and white cherry on top of each scoop.

SLANG USED

Slanguage of the 1930s
https://www.smokyhillmuseum.org/file_download/in-line/9e42437b-e940-4eb9-962b-dd66163d451c

Slang of the 30s
https://www.pinterest.com/pin/slang-of-the-1930s--68539225558850276/

Abercrombie: a real know-it-all; taken from Slang of the 1930s

Cabbage or *Lettuce:* money

Dollface: a pretty girl

English Drape suits: "The English Drape cut is a style for single breasted and double breasted jackets or topcoats featuring fullness across the chest, forming vertical wrinkles, as well as over the shoulder blades." www. GentlemansGazette.com/drape-cut/

Glad eye: happy to see someone

Gumshoe: or flatfoot; a detective

Jeffersons: twenty-dollar bills

Kansas City Shuffle: a scam game where the scammer gets the patsy (or victim) to think one thing where they are involved in a get rich quick scheme and then turn the tables and their money is taken. A good example can be found in the movie *The Sting*.

Rear back in a chair: sitting in a chair with the front two legs in the air.

Ring off: to disconnect a call. The old hand crank telephones required a person to turn the crank and the end of a conversation to disconnect the call, thus notifying the operator that the call ended. The term remained in use even after the crank telephones were no longer used.

Skirt: girl

Stepping out: going out on a date or to dance

Trip the Lights Fantastic: partying and dancing

Miss Markham Mysteries

BOOK TWO

Why does Deloris make an emergency trip up to Jameson? What was found after a tornado hit? What happens next in Deloris's life?

Check out Miss Markham's next book, *Deadly Peculiarities at the Jameson Picnic*, for those answers and more.

Prologue

THE BANDSTAND

I
t was never a good sign when the sky turned dark on a summer afternoon in Northwest Missouri, Maude Fine thought, looking warily upwards. As she kept watch, the clouds had changed from white fluff balls to grey rainclouds, and then into a dark green, angry, swirling mass as evening arrived early. Into the eerie stillness, as the birds stopped singing, a sound like thunder emerged. It grew louder and louder until it sounded like a train roaring in towards the depot. But no train was due, and Maude and all the residents of Jameson knew what that sound was as they hurried to take shelter. A tornado was coming and, by the sound of it, a bad one.

Playing a giant game of hopscotch, the tornado touched down, lifted up, and then touched down again to the accompaniment of moaning winds and cracking trees. Eventually the destructive storm moved on and the night became peaceful.

Early the next morning, Maude and her husband, Jameson mayor Tom Fine, went for a drive to see what the storm had done. They weren't the only ones keen to survey the damage; the residents of Jameson were out in full force to clear trees and take stock of what needed to be repaired. Luckily, most of the tornado's dance had been in fields north of town, with the houses in Jameson spared except for a few missing shingles and broken windows.

Tom and Maude pulled to a stop by City Park, where the bandstand had taken a direct hit from a falling oak tree and had collapsed completely.

"There's no fixing that," Maude said.

"No," her husband shook his head. "It'll have to be rebuilt."

Maude waved as Nellie and Owen Robertson approached from the other direction on Chestnut Street. Owen stopped his sedan across from the Fine's car and leaned out of his window. Tom did the same and Nellie leaned across Owen towards the open window.

"Can you get the bandstand put up again in time?" Nellie asked Tom. "The picnic is only five weeks away."

"I reckon so," Tom replied. "I'm going to call Old Man Jones to see what can be done."

"Good," Nellie said. "If anyone can get it built in time, he can."

"Just tell Old Man Jones to build it as quickly as he talks," Maude said to her husband with a twinkle in her eye. "It'll be up in no time."

Later that morning, Emmett "Old Man" Jones pulled up to the bandstand in his 1926 Model TT Ford pickup with his dog Rex on the seat beside him. Old Man Jones was well-known throughout Daviess County for the quality of his construction work and the quantity of his words. The mayor was waiting for him and the two men walked over to the bandstand.

"Can you rebuild it by the picnic?" Tom asked.

"Don't you worry none," Emmett replied. "The Jameson Picnic has been meeting on this weekend for the past thirty-nine years and I don't aim to let one little tornado stop it now."

"Good," the mayor said, looking relieved. "The picnic wouldn't be the same without it."

"Bart and Corny are on their way," Emmett continued. "I had them stop at the lumberyard to place an order for what we'll need. The planks for the stage and the roof should be easy enough to get, but I wasn't sure if they'd have them big timbers we need for the supports. And everybody's out buying shingles today, thanks to that dern storm. We won't need 'em until we get the rest of the bandstand built, but I wanted to git our order in to make sure they'd have 'em when we need 'em." Emmett gestured towards the wreckage of the tree and the bandstand. "We'll have all this mess taken out before sundown or my name ain't Emmett Meriweather Jones. Should be able to start rebuilding tomorrow, iffen one of the hardware stores in this here town has got everything else we need. An iffen they don't, I'll send Bart and Corny over to Pattonsburg. That is, if Bart's old jalopy don't break down. That car is held together by bailing twine and bull—" Emmett stopped abruptly, remembering who he was talking to.

"I'll tell everyone the picnic will go ahead as scheduled," the mayor said, trying to find a way to end the conversation.

"Yessir," Emmett said. "I'll get a new bandstand up lickety-split, ready for the talent show and baby contest, baking contest, an' all the bands—plus the place for you to speak from, of course." He licked his lips at the memory of past picnics when he entered the pie-eating and watermelon-eating contest and had a tenderloin followed with more homemade pie. "No siree, can't have the picnic without the bandstand," he continued, "but it's an easy job. No need to install windows or walls, just rebuild the stage and put a roof over it to block the sun. Nothing to gum up the works." Emmett pointed to a smaller building, ten feet away. "And the tree didn't even take out the cookshack, that woulda been a bigger job, what with the kitchen equipment and all. I'm just glad I caught Craig Ness at his farm 'fore I come over here. He should be here soon."

"Why is Craig coming?" the mayor asked, interested in spite of himself.

"Didn't ya hear? He just bought hisself a new Farmall F30 tractor from over in Gallatin. It's still shiny an' everything. That oak tree ain't an acorn, you know? Figure we can pull it away with the tractor faster'n trying to saw it up into pieces to move. You should hear that engine go—it's got enough power to pull anything. I brought chains to attach the tree to the tractor; they're in the back of my truck. Craig's gonna pull the tree across the tree line to O'Casey's barn, and cut it up fer firewood there. O'Casey is an ol' devil but I talked him into letting us move everything over there." Old Man Jones gave a toothy grin, and continued, "I told him the entire citizenry of Jameson would be lathered up at him iffen he didn't. He don't want to get on the bad side of the biddies. Meaning no disrespect to your missus, Mayor, but them ladies can be a might scary when they get riled. And we'll move what's left of the old bandstand there, too, and whoever wants the scraps can pick 'em up themselves. Then—"

Rex interrupted the conversation, barking from the pickup at the rumbling arrival of Craig Ness on his tractor. Jones stopped talking for a second to wave at Craig, and seizing his chance, the mayor quickly said, "I'll leave everything in your hands. Good day, Emmett." He offered a handshake and then walked away while Old Man Jones started in talking to Craig about the finer points of the new tractor.

Bart and Corny, Old Man Jones' hired hands, arrived with a rattle in a dusty old jalopy just as Craig's tractor made short work of hauling away the tree. Once the tree was gone, it was time to start removing the debris from the bandstand. Rex, who had been kept inside the pickup so that he wouldn't be underfoot while the tractor was working, leapt out as soon as Emmett untied him and opened the door. The dog relieved himself as soon as his feet touched the ground and then ran over to greet Bart and Corny where they stood, looking at the squashed roof of the bandstand. Once there, however, the hound seemed to abandon his greeting, and instead started sniffing determinedly.

"You smell somethin', boy?" Emmett asked.

"Prob'ly just a ground squirrel," Bart opined.

Rex picked up a trail and followed it to the far edge of the destroyed bandstand where the floor had come up, pulling with it the posts that had secured the bandstand into the earth for thirty-nine years. Rex began rooting through the boards and debris with his nose and paws. He used his jaws to pick up a board and move it to one side, and then moved another. Eventually, he got through the debris to bare ground and began digging.

"Fool dog," Emmett said fondly. "We got to get to work, Rex, and you don't need no rabbit or bone."

Emmett went over to pull the dog away from his quest so that they could start work. Just as he reached down to grab the rope he used as a collar on the dog, he stopped. There at Rex's feet were bones all right, in the shape of a human hand.

"Tarnation!" was the only word the came from his mouth. For the first time in his life, Old Man Jones was speechless.

"What the...?" was the only response Corny managed to get out when he walked over and saw the cream-colored bones resting in the shallow depression Rex had dug.

"Boss, is that a hand?" Bart asked.

Emmett Jones nodded, still unable to speak. After a moment he told Bart, "Run over to Frankie Martin's house and call the sheriff." "I'm gonna stay here with Corny."

Bart nodded in reply, but then he stopped and asked, "Isn't Miz Martin in that new telephone building?"

"Oh, dern it, yes, I mean go to the telephone building and ask her to call the sheriff. I fergit she just moved in there last week. Now git."

Then Old Man Jones looked at Corny and added, "put Rex back into the truck and tie him up, he don't need to do no more digging today."

www.ingramcontent.com/pod-product-compliance
Lightning Source LLC
Chambersburg PA
CBHW020311200626
46814CB00006BA/2197